5/

VENGEANCE
TASTES SWEET

VENGEANCE
TASTES SWEET

•

Joani Ascher

AVALON BOOKS
NEW YORK

PRINTED IN THE UNITED STATES OF AMERICA
ON ACID-FREE PAPER
BY HADDON CRAFTSMEN, BLOOMSBURG, PENNSYLVANIA

For my son, Ari, a word meister extraordinaire,
and my daughter, Shonna, who knows far too much
about poison,
and my husband, David, whose reputation precedes him,
with all my love.

Acknowledgments

My most grateful thanks to Jane Degnan, Deborah Nolan, Mary Elizabeth Allen, and Kim Zito, as well as Fredericka Glucksman, Mark Podolsky and Nancy Janow. I would also like to thank my brother Stephen Wolf, for answering my questions, my family, for their editorial assistance, and my editor, Erin Cartwright.

Prologue

Beverly Cohen hurried upstairs. She hated to leave her guests and her oh-so-successful party but she had to get to the bathroom. The powder room in the foyer would never do.

She felt so strange. Her husband, Doug, would be angry that she had left him with all those guests, but she just had to get upstairs. It was as simple as that.

This party must be too much for her, she thought, although that didn't make sense. She'd handled many other parties before, both in her home and elsewhere.

Once Beverly reached the huge marble bathroom, she considered splashing water on her face, which felt warm. But she decided not to because it would ruin her makeup. She inspected herself from the many angles provided by the multiple mirrors. She didn't look bad. Her face was so pink she positively glowed. But all her lipstick was gone. She pursed her lips, wondering how long that sad state of affairs had existed.

A numb sensation seemed to extend from her lips to her tongue.

The bathroom was oppressively warm so Bev headed across her bedroom, aiming for her bed. Strangely, it almost felt as if she were walking through deep sand.

Doug should be able to handle things downstairs, she

reasoned. Many of the people had already left, certainly all the important ones. It had been wonderful having those movie stars in her home. It certainly showed everyone how important and successful she was, especially Janet. Her old friend had been nearly speechless with admiration, Bev was sure. Every time she caught her eye, Janet had looked away with humiliation at how much better her old roommate had done with her life. They may have been college roommates but they were very different—Bev was always destined for greatness and Janet was, well, Janet. What could she expect?

Most of the rest of Beverly's guests, those dull and dreary people who were her neighbors in town, were on the way out the door when she ran past them up the steps. They had all smiled politely when she tried to stammer out a good-bye, which had been kind of frustrating and embarrassing.

She didn't usually have trouble talking.

In fact, she sometimes had the impression that people wished she wouldn't talk so much. But she had so much to say. Her life was filled with fabulous and interesting events. Not being able to say a simple good-bye was weird. Luckily it hadn't been anyone important anyway.

Her legs felt leaden, as if she were dragging through the carpet. She had really overdone it, serving and cooking and everything, practically all by herself. Those witches the agency had sent had been so inappropriate, she wasn't sorry that they left after only a few minutes. But then she was left with all that work! She'd had to cover her $1,500 Versace dress with an apron, one that advertised her catering business, of course, but still. And her $400 Manolo Blahniks hadn't exactly been the most comfortable shoes she could have worn, what with all that running around.

It was a good thing that she had reconciled with Nancy, since Nancy had really helped. Maybe, Bev thought, she shouldn't have let the partnership go, but Nancy wasn't on the same fast track. She didn't want to cater to the rich and famous. She'd settle for working for the semi-rich and very-boring.

Somehow Bev got across the palatial room to her king-sized satin-covered bed. It was good to lie on the down-filled comforter. She reflected on the day. All those people, right there in her kitchen. And they had talked to her, shared with her, both stories and food. It was a dream come true.

Now that she was lying down she felt a little better, although for some reason she was having trouble breathing. *Too much excitement*, she told herself, *calm down*. Since her body felt so heavy and so numb and it was such a strain to move, she rested.

Time seemed to slide by and the room got dark while she floated along. Suddenly, however, Beverly started to shake uncontrollably. It was impossible to stop shaking, to catch her breath, to . . .

Blackness enveloped her.

Several hours after the Grosvenor, New Jersey, Rescue Squad and the doctors in the emergency room had made frantic attempts to revive her, Beverly Cohen, aged thirty-four, was pronounced dead at the hospital. She had never regained consciousness.

Nancy Goldstein, aged twenty-eight, a former partner of Cohen, was arrested sometime later.

Chapter One

Wally Morris heard people complaining as soon as she left the director's office after the budget meeting.

"You'd think she'd have more sense than to park in the driveway when we have to get our kids home," said a woman herding three children out the synagogue door.

"Who did that?" asked a man with a little boy who still wore his yarmulke, a rule for the boys in the school, since Jewish males were required to keep their heads covered.

Someone else pointed toward the synagogue kitchen. Wally saw the retreating figure in jeans, boots, and a full-length mink coat, of Beverly Cohen.

"Oh, her," said another woman. "She doesn't care about anyone but herself. If she doesn't hurry, Marissa is going to be late for ballet. Her mother will kill me."

The man said he would go talk to the director to get him to tell Beverly to move her car immediately. Wally turned to find that Marissa was the same child who had been in her nursery school class several years earlier, and used the time to chat with her and three other former students. Two of them were already taller than she, but that was to be expected. Wally had to look up to see five feet.

By the time she got outside, she saw a huge line of cars

4

waiting for the Hebrew School students. Shaking her head, Wally pulled out of her parking spot, and took her place behind them.

It was nearly 5:40 and she wasn't done with her evening's errands. Luckily, she had partially defrosted the frozen manicotti that she'd made the week before. It was now in the oven, and the automatic timer had started cooking it at 5:15. It would be ready when she returned. All she needed to do was pick up a French bread and throw together a salad. If she timed it right, her husband, Nate, might even get the salad done before she got home.

Never one to sit idly, Wally tried to use the time to sort through some balls of yarn she had picked up. But it was difficult in the dark. She gave up and flicked on an all-news radio station, hoping to catch a weather report.

A female voice crooned about a benefit scheduled for later that evening. "Hollywood will be turning out in New York tonight," she said, "as the world of film takes time off from its busy pre-Christmas rush to release those holiday movies we've all been waiting for. They'll be just in time to be in the running for this year's Oscars. Tonight's event is a benefit for AIDS research and all the big names will be there—Tom Hanks, Julia Roberts, Michael Douglas, Steven Spielberg, Heath Maxwell, and Melanie Jensen. This glittering gala will be held in the Waldorf Astoria where the thousand-dollar-a-plate dinner promises more than just salad. We'll have an update on this later, and I promise to tell you absolutely all about it tomorrow. This is Maggie Faulkner, in New York."

The voice of the regular radio announcer thanked Maggie, as if she were listening, and went into another story. "People in the little New Jersey town of Grosvenor will be rubbing elbows in a few months with several of the guests at tonight's benefit. Covering that story for us is Peter Marsh. What have you got, Pete?"

"Well, Harry, it seems that the New Jersey Film Commission has been successful in packaging Grosvenor as the perfect place to shoot director Skip Runyon's next film,

Stalking Sunrise. Shooting is scheduled to begin in February and run through spring."

"That's good news," Harry said. "I'm sure the people in that town will be very excited to hear it. Thanks, Pete."

Wally got goosebumps. She had heard there was a possibility of the movie being filmed in town, but hadn't really believed it. She felt a huge sense of pride and couldn't wait to talk about it with Nate. Unfortunately, that didn't look like it was going to happen any time soon.

The line of cars still wasn't moving. Wally was directly behind a mini-van which was nearly bouncing due to the five unattended children inside rapidly decompressing from two hours of Hebrew School.

After several more minutes the carpool line finally began to move. It was almost six o'clock and Wally had visions of blackened manicotti.

Beverly Cohen's diamond-studded watch said that it was almost eight o'clock and Doug still hadn't come back to his posh Park Avenue office. Beverly was supposed to meet him there a half-hour earlier so he could take her to the benefit. Nearly beside herself with excitement, she was having a tough time not picking at her $75 manicure, especially since she'd heard the news about her town being the location site for that new movie. She would have sat on her hands, but there was also the little problem that she didn't want to sit down, because then her incredibly tight, floor-length, fire-engine-red dress might wrinkle.

She knew she had the body for it. At five-foot-eight, one-hundred-ten-pounds, she looked pretty good for thirty-four. Her legs went from the floor to just below her ears, or so Doug always joked. Well, used to joke, anyway. It seemed like now he was just too busy for everything, including jokes. Where was he anyway?

The phone buzzed, and Beverly picked it up. It didn't matter at all to her that this was Doug's office, not hers. She pretty much did what she wanted in there.

"Yes?" she said into the receiver.

"Oh, Bev," Doug said, slightly out of breath. "I'm glad you're there. I was worried that you'd be late."

After what she went through to get there on time, she was miffed with his implication. "Why would I be late?"

"Well, I, uh, I thought you might have trouble parking the car. The traffic in the city is so bad right now."

"I took a limo."

There was a significant pause on the line. Too bad if he doesn't like it, Bev thought. I make enough money to afford it. Not, of course, that I'd take the expense out of my own money. Doug could afford it too, considering the only patients he saw were terrifically rich. None of that Medicaid or even Medicare for him.

"I'll be there in fifteen minutes," Doug said evenly.

"Where are you? And why aren't you here now? The benefit starts in less than half an hour and I do not—do you understand me, Douglas—do not want to be late."

"I'll get there faster if you let me get off the phone."

Before Beverly could ask him another question he had hung up. She looked around her husband's office for a magazine but all she saw were patient files. Sighing, she sat down to read.

Lights flashed, nearly blinding Beverly as she and Doug watched the rich and famous entering the Waldorf. It was so exciting that she had to remind herself to keep breathing when several of the stars nodded hello to her husband. When Ashley Noelle stopped in front of them and actually called Doug by name, Bev had to grab onto his elbow to keep from falling off her four-and-a-half-inch spike heels. She could barely utter a response when Doug introduced her to the leading lady in the latest Skip Runyon movie, *The Devil's Quarry*.

They were swept inside the hotel on a tide of onlookers. Once inside, they had to produce their tickets to prove to the officious doorman that they, two total unknowns, were entitled to enter the ballroom. He seemed to be inspecting the pieces of cardboard to make sure that they weren't counterfeit, and it annoyed Doug. He got that set to his shoulders that signaled trouble.

"Don't worry, sweetheart," Bev soothed. "If you come to enough of these, and get more patients, soon you'll be well known. Maybe we'll even get an invitation to the White House."

Doug's face didn't lose its tension, but his shoulders did. The danger was past. Bev turned away and looked around.

It was more spectacular than she could ever have imagined. If she tried, she could bump elbows with some of the most famous people in the world. Her best hope was that they would at least notice that she was there, but she had plans to make it more than that, at least with a few of them. Doug wasn't the only one hoping to capitalize on the break that now led him to be associated with some of these people. At least half of them had homes in New York, New Jersey, and Connecticut, and they just might need her catering services.

Elliot Levine knew there was no way out.

His girlfriend, Debbie, had decided that she had to stop off at her parents' house to pick up a few things she needed for her apartment in New York before going to spend the evening studying at Elliot's. Since they lived so close, it was supposed to take only a few minutes. But Debbie's mother, Wally Morris, had just come home, complaining about some traffic tie-up. She complained while she took off her jacket and hung it on a hook, and while she took Debbie's and Elliot's jackets and hung up theirs. She went on 'and on, which reminded Elliot of his meeting that morning.

Captain Jaeger, his boss at the Grosvenor Police Department where Elliot was a detective, had called everyone to the briefing room. The meeting was held as soon as the news was confirmed that Grosvenor had been selected as the filming site of that movie. The officers were all under strict curtailment of free time, and everyone was expected to work as many hours of overtime as it took to make sure that the filming went smoothly. Jaeger topped off his long-winded lecture with his usual, I'll-accept-no-excuses warning. When everyone was ready to leave the room, Jaeger had added, "I want traffic tie-ups avoided," as if that were possible, considering how many cars, trucks, vans, and equipment would be moving into town.

Elliot passed along the warning to Mrs. Morris. "Traffic will be worse when they start filming that movie."

"I'll keep that in mind," she said, as she pulled on her oven mitts. She took a quick look in the oven, "To see if dinner survived," as she put it.

"It's okay," she said, turning to Elliot and Debbie. "Would you care to join us? I have plenty."

Although it meant it would take longer to get Debbie to his house, Elliot heard Debbie accept the offer. That was okay with him, since Mrs. Morris was a great cook. She had a reputation for always cooking huge quantities of food, even though only she and her husband lived in the house most of the time. Debbie's older sister, Rachel, was married with a family of her own. Their brother, Mark, a sophomore at Princeton, was away at school. Yet Mrs. Morris cooked like they were all expected for dinner.

"This movie is going to put Grosvenor on the map," said Mr. Morris.

"As the headache capital of the world," Elliot said quietly.

"Did you say something?" Mrs. Morris asked.

"Er, no." Elliot knew that the Morrises were excited about the filming. They had mentioned it three times since he walked through the door.

"Don't be so negative," Debbie said. "It'll be fun."

So she was in their corner, Elliot thought. Sure, it wouldn't affect the amount of time she had to study for her law courses. She didn't have a full-time job on top of being in law school. He turned to look at her, thinking he might point that out, but she looked too delicious to contradict, in her turtleneck sweater and jeans. Besides, the few weeks of filming would probably be okay. He hadn't worried about it at all until he saw Captain Jaeger's reaction, and he had to admit, the captain was not known for being calm. His motto, according to Elliot's partner, was: Overreact first and think about it later.

Mrs. Morris put onto his plate stuffed manicotti covered in sauce and cheese. It smelled so good that he was salivating. And it wasn't only about the food. After a week of not seeing Debbie because she was tied up working on her moot court presentations, he had looked forward to spending time with her. He would lose himself in her blue-green eyes, run his fingers through her blond hair, and kiss her for a while, before hitting the books. And afterwards, maybe again.

His thoughts were interrupted by a basket of bread passing under his nose. "Would you like some?" Mr. Morris asked.

"Yes, please." He took a big slice of the crusty semolina bread and passed the basket to Debbie.

"Do you want any more to eat?" Mrs. Morris asked her husband a while later, as he wiped his plate with a piece of bread.

"I don't think so," he said. "It was wonderful, as usual. I like that crusty top." He got up, his lean, six-foot frame towering over his wife, and cut some more bread.

Elliot knew that ordinarily, Mr. Morris wore jeans or chinos and a sweater to his office, which was in the barn behind the house. He had both his businesses in that renovated barn. One was an investment agency, for which he also published a newsletter, and the other was an insurance business he'd inherited from his father and ran for his widowed mother. The office was quite comfortable, in a rustic way. But tonight Mr. Morris had an apron over his striped button-down shirt and pleated suit pants. Elliot assumed he'd had a business meeting in Manhattan.

Mrs. Morris giggled at her husband's remark. "That was a delicate way of saying the casserole was overdone." She turned and looked pointedly at Elliot, as if making sure he noticed how a good husband would handle a problem like that. Out loud she said, "Would you like some more?"

"No, thanks," he said. Elliot often felt that Debbie's mother, a very sharp woman, was waiting for something, such as a big announcement.

Debbie turned down another helping as well. Both of them had seen the cake that Mrs. Morris pulled out of the freezer when they walked through the door, and Elliot knew Debbie wanted to save room for it.

He watched as she got up to help clear the table. When she stood next to her mother, who still looked quite young even though she was almost fifty, Debbie was a bit taller, at about five feet. Her light coloring was different too, since Mrs. Morris had brown hair and eyes. The two women worked together in an easy way, and Elliot found himself fantasizing about standing next to Debbie like that, in his own kitchen.

When the tea kettle whistled, Mrs. Morris walked around Sammy, their black Labrador retriever, who was sprawled on the kitchen floor. He wagged his tail hopefully, waiting patiently for a dog biscuit. He didn't take his eyes off her for a second as she poured the water into the waiting cups.

Mrs. Morris laughed, went over to the pantry, and got out a dog cookie. "Here you go," she said, tossing it. The biscuit never hit the floor.

The cake, which had nearly come up to room temperature, was an orange-chocolate pound loaf. Elliot ate it slowly, savoring every bite. It occurred to him, though, that the sooner they finished eating, the sooner he and Debbie could leave, so he picked up the pace. He tried to catch Debbie's eye, to see if she was ready to go.

They were all set to make their escape when Mr. Morris spoke up. "Did you see the local paper today?" he asked.

Elliot and Debbie both shook their heads.

"Was there anything accurate in it?" Mrs. Morris asked.

Mr. Morris chuckled. "Actually, yes." He looked at Elliot. "They finally got around to reporting on those commendations that you and Dominique received last month."

Elliot was surprised. He and his partner, Dominique

Scott, had lost hope of media recognition for the work they did. "What did they say?"

"They called you fine detectives," Mr. Morris said. "They even made a reference to the first commendations you got after that incident last year."

Mrs. Morris smiled. "Finally."

"You mean you aren't still trying to take credit for helping them solve the murder and kidnapping?" Debbie asked her mother.

"Of course not."

Elliot knew well enough that if not for Mrs. Morris, it might never have been solved. Although she declined any mention of her involvement to outsiders, many people in town knew about it.

Debbie came to stand beside Elliot's chair, and gave his shoulder a squeeze. He reached up and took her hand, thanking her for the vote of confidence. She had a way of easing all of his self-doubts. The thought of marrying her crossed his mind frequently, although he wasn't yet ready to make a public commitment. He knew that Debbie shared his understanding. When he finished law school this spring, she'd still have a year to go. An engagement then would make sense. It seemed inevitable, to Elliot at least. Debbie was the woman to spend his life with. She was beautiful, smart, sensible, and he loved her to his core. With her, he could be himself, and bask in the glow of her love. But he would ask her in his own time, not according to her mother's timetable.

Beverly was frustrated. No one famous would talk to her. She went over to the bar and got another drink. It was only her third gin and tonic, or was it her fourth? They made them so strong here.

She stood next to a large ficus plant and watched how the rich and famous moved, nodding to this one or that, ignoring others. Unfortunately, she was among the ignorees, far more than Doug. He was doing fairly well, and had been engaged in several conversations with people whom Beverly was dying to meet. But she didn't dare butt in. Hopefully he was drumming up more business, and she'd eventually get to meet those people.

A fabulous-looking man, whom Bev was sure was in the last Emma Thompson movie, came straight toward her, smiling. "How are you?" he asked, extending his hand.

Bev reached out her own for his handshake, while stammering, "F-fine." But he walked right past her and shook hands with another man behind her.

She hoped her face wasn't really on fire, although that's exactly what it felt like.

Feeling totally embarrassed, and a bit drunk, Beverly turned to see who was standing next to her, breathing on her bare elbow. To her surprise she discovered a man, several inches shorter than she, looking up at her, holding a plate brimming with canapés. Bev figured he was about forty, but he was not dressed like the beautiful people. His tux didn't quite fit and she could see that his cuffs were frayed when he held another canapé in his hand.

"Hello. My name is Beverly Cohen," she said. He wasn't someone she recognized, but he could be an agent, or a producer, or an eccentric director. That would explain the way he was dressed. She put on a charming smile, and went over in her mind how she would explain her presence at the event, if the subject came up. It would be a good time to plug Doug.

"Hi," he replied. "I'm Tad."

"Those canapés look delish," she said, plucking one off his plate and into her mouth.

He smiled. "So what brings you here?"

Bev straightened up, ready to tell him. If she could make it interesting enough, maybe he'd stick around.

Tad Seymour, a moniker more acceptable than his real name, Hyman Seltzer, rushed back to his office. He wished he could afford to take a cab, but he'd maxed out his credit cards on the ticket to the AIDS benefit, in the wild hopes that he could get some juicy information that he could parlay into big money. Yet the temptation to splurge was great, almost overwhelming, because he had hit paydirt.

He could see the headlines forming in his mind. These would edge out the latest sightings of Bigfoot, and the babies who had given birth to their own mothers. This was huge and could turn the world on its ear. It was explosive information and it was actually true. Maybe. And that half-drunk, beanpole blond lady who had given it to him didn't even know who she was talking to. She went on and on, oblivious to the stares of people around her, talking and stuffing her face with the food from his plate. She followed him to the tables of food as he refilled his plate, all the while chattering on. It was lucky for him that they talked before he stepped on the hem of her red dress, ripping an eight-inch piece of the fabric. Her shrieking had made him drop his third plate of goodies. Worse than that, every head in the room had turned their way.

The only thing he needed was corroboration. There had been too many successful lawsuits lately, like the one that had cost him his job. Tad was sure the tidbit was true, there was no reason to doubt it, but he wouldn't be able to make a cent off this story without something more. He laughed to himself. The best defense against a claim of libel was truth. And if this was true, well, people would find it astounding. It might even change someone's life.

Chapter Two

Wally shivered as she went through the doors of the temple. It was a cold, gray, rainy December afternoon, one meant for sitting at home with a book and a second cup of coffee. But she had promised Toby that she would help bake for the rabbi's party.

Through the glass wall of the office, Wally could see the rabbi on the phone talking to someone. She wondered if he was excited about the testimonial dinner, $75 a plate no less, that was being held in his and the rebbetzin's honor. It was hard to believe that it was already twenty years since he had become the rabbi of the synagogue. He'd presided over Wally's three children's b'nai mitzvot, when they came of age, Jewishly speaking, and were first called to the Torah. The rabbi had also performed Rachel's wedding ceremony, and had conducted Wally's mother's and Nate's father's funerals.

With a wave, Wally passed the office and headed for the kitchen. Toby would be waiting for Wally to work some magic on the ten cakes that she had promised to make.

By the time she got there, the kitchen was full of people busily preparing for the party. Wally saw, to her dismay, that Beverly Cohen was cooking, and she had several people helping her. She was known for donating her time and expertise to the synagogue, but the woman had a tendency to get on Wally's nerves.

"Wally!" said Toby, a large, pleasant-faced woman wearing a big, lime-green apron and a frazzled expression. "I'm so glad you're here." She smiled while she showed Wally where to set up and which mixer to use, but her face looked strained, and Wally thought she could use a break.

"Toby, could you show me something in the meat kitchen?" Wally asked.

"The party is dairy," Beverly said, as if Wally was some kind of kashruth ignoramus and didn't know how to keep kosher, "so there will be no meat. We can't mix milk and meat according to Jewish law."

Next, Wally thought, Beverly would explain that pork and shellfish weren't kosher either, that they were considered traif, unclean, and not to be eaten. Wally had been keeping her own kosher kitchen since the age of eleven, when her grandmother died. Her mother, who had never recovered from the loss of Wally's father, had always deferred to her own mother in the kitchen, and deferred to her daughter once the old woman was gone. Most people didn't find it necessary to explain the rules of kashruth to Wally.

With a supreme effort to control her temper, Wally said, "This is for something else." It annoyed her that she had to look up to speak to Bev, who for some reason was wearing three-inch heels to cook, as if she wasn't tall enough to begin with. She was also wearing fawn-colored silk slacks, and a matching silk-and-ramie-blend sweater with decorative sequins. The outfit was partially covered by an apron that proclaimed her to be Top Chef, and her blond hair was blown dry, poofed, and sprayed into place like a helmet.

Wally resisted the urge to run her fingers through her own short, sable mist-colored hair, and to bend under the left side which always, willfully, flipped up. Even if she were only in her mid-thirties like Bev, her hair would never look like Top Chef's.

Toby smiled at Wally. "Yes. I'd be happy to show you something in the meat kitchen." She turned to the others in the room and said in a general way, "We'll be right back." Then she took Wally by the arm and hurried her out of the room.

When they were out of earshot, Toby slowed down. "Thanks for giving me a chance to get out of there. She's driving me crazy. It's been one thing after another, and I'm the one responsible for this."

There was no need for Wally to ask who Toby was talking about. "So what exactly is Beverly doing?"

"She's changing everything. First she decided that there aren't going to be any latkes, even though it will still be Chanukah. She said that it's too déclassé to serve them. I don't really care, but the older ladies are expecting them, and they'll make a fuss if they don't get what they expect."

Wally nodded. Toby was right. Some of the congregants could get very loud when expressing their surprise at changes that were made without their knowledge. It would be downright embarrassing to hear them go on and on. "What is she going to serve instead?"

"Oh, you'll love this. She got some recipe for some special kind of southern sweet potato or something. It costs fifty percent more than a normal one. And she's going to cook up tons of it. She says it is supposed to be the sweetest thing around. That way, according to her, they'll get their potatoes."

"But that still won't be potato pancakes. No one will think it is latkes. I thought that was one of the reasons that the testimonial was put off until Chanukah. You can stretch latkes and applesauce a long way."

Toby shook her head. "Not now. Now we're having these potatoes and filet of flounder rolled around salmon."

"Is that in your budget?"

"No. It's way over budget. But Bev sold everyone on the idea and now we have to do it. It'll be covered, we're charging enough for that, but it'll come out of the gift for the rabbi and his wife, and that will make me look bad."

Wally felt sorry for her friend. "I guess we have to go back and face the music," she said. "I'll get the cakes done without bothering you too much."

"Thanks," Toby said, looking a little better since she'd unburdened herself. "Oh, I forgot to tell you, I lined up a helper for you. Louise Fisch."

"Great," Wally said, unable to keep from chuckling over the pleasant surprise. Louise was her best friend. "That's nice. It'll make this go faster."

They walked back into the kitchen in the middle of a story that Beverly was telling. "Everywhere you looked there was another celebrity. And I had this long conversation with someone who I'm sure is absolutely famous, even though I didn't recognize his name. Tad something, I think. And the food was okay, even if I could have made it better myself."

Bev looked over at someone who was trying to drain a huge pot of pasta over the sink. "You'd better watch out," she warned. "I heard about a man who was working in a restaurant and burned his chest with hot water. It ruined his chances for underwear ads."

Wally suppressed a laugh behind a bag of flour. It was clear to her that Bev was talking out of school. Nate would have killed her if she told the details of anyone's investments or insurance policies, and Bev was telling people about far more private things, things that her husband the doctor was required to keep confidential.

"Oh, Marianne," Bev said. "Cut those peppers smaller. We want them diced evenly. They look so much better that way. I had hoped my housekeeper could do that, but I needed her to stay home today. I'm expecting a large delivery."

Marianne Sachs, wearing one of her trademark floor-length dresses, looked around the room for reassurance. Wally smiled sympathetically at her. She was a nice woman, and didn't deserve Bev's harsh and patronizing tones.

Toby looked as if she wanted to find a job for Marianne

to make her feel better after Bev's comments, but didn't know what to assign. Wally felt sorry for her.

"Erin," Bev said, turning her attention to a new victim, "I know you aren't familiar with how this kitchen works. Make sure you ask me if you have any questions. You can stand over there to cut the celery."

The look on Erin Feldman's chubby face was nothing short of astonished. Her already huge blue eyes were wide as she turned bright red, and she pressed her lips together so hard that Wally thought her bottom jaw would end up on top. Wally knew for a fact that Erin kept a strictly kosher kitchen at home, so kosher in fact that the rabbi never hesitated to accept a dinner invitation when his wife was away. Since Erin had converted to Judaism as a teenager, few people had ever questioned her authenticity, until Bev. It was a horrid thing to say and Wally suspected that Bev knew that quite well.

Another woman who was present shook her close-cropped head, causing her long delicate earrings to shake. Nancy Goldstein, Bev's former partner in the catering business, appeared to be used to Beverly's obnoxious tone. She stood with her back toward Bev but she clearly felt sorry for the others who were being exposed to it for the first time. She looked miserably at Wally.

In general, Nancy seemed to mind her own business and stay well away from Bev. She didn't comment on any of the goings on in the kitchen. It was quite a contrast to how she had been the year before, when she and Bev were still friendly and in business together.

Nancy had agreed to help with the party only as a favor to Toby. She was in charge of organizing beverages and punch mixes, and fixing a huge multi-tiered fruit platter.

For her part, Wally noticed that Bev avoided Nancy. It had been a bitter split, according to the grapevine. Nancy, at least partially because of her youth and naiveté, had been edged out of the partnership without a penny exchanging hands. Wally knew that she'd made an enormous capital investment when the business was first starting up, and it didn't seem fair. When Nate wrote the five-year insurance policy on the venture, they were listed as equal partners. Beverly had seen to it that they were each insured for a lot of money, as if she were worth millions. In fact, the way the policy was written, if Bev died, Nancy would get twice as much as Bev would if Nancy died. That was arrogance.

Rumor had it that someone had become ill at one of the parties the two women catered. Somehow Nancy had been held singularly responsible. It wasn't even clear if it was a food-related illness, but Beverly's husband, who had treated the victim, diagnosed food poisoning. Beverly blamed Nancy, and even though there was no proof, and no one else became ill, they dissolved the partnership. Nancy, whose husband was out of the country on business at the time, hired a lawyer but still ended up with nothing. If it weren't for her husband's job, they would have been in very difficult financial straits.

Wally turned her back on the group and began to measure out ingredients for a chocolate chip pound cake. Because they were not serving a meat meal she could use real butter, and she knew the cake would be delicious. She'd never had a failure with it. She also had to grate lemon rinds for the poppyseed cake. Hopefully Louise would be there to help.

"Thank goodness you're here," Wally said to Louise while she was tying her apron over her yellow knit dress. "I've been going out of my mind."

Louise finished putting a barrette into her fiery red hair to hold it back, and glanced over at Beverly. "I see your problem. But it was my turn to work the phones at the office. And I think I picked up a new client. Even with what happened last year, people are still interested in moving to Grosvenor."

Wally grimaced. She didn't need to be reminded about the trouble.

"So what's cooking?" Louise asked.

"Let's get another set of cakes ready to bake," Wally

said, "and then I'll fill you in." She dropped her voice. "But don't be surprised if you get insulted while we're working." She looked over at Beverly to indicate who would be the source of the insult.

Louise followed her gaze. "What's the scoop?" she whispered.

"Among other things, she had a child in one of my nursery school classes one year. The little girl was only one-and-a-half, and there was Bev insisting that she had to go to school five days a week, even though we had the class for the under-twos only on Thursday and Friday. The mothers have to stay in the class when they are that age, and people can't do it every morning. So we put her into the two-and-a-half-year-old class, where she really didn't belong, and told Beverly that she would have to be present every day, or that she'd have to keep the child home."

"I can't picture the director allowing Bev to push her around like that," Louise said.

Wally nodded. "So you'd think. But the Cohens are big contributors to the temple, particularly the nursery school. Our director didn't want to see those dollars come out of her budget."

"So did it work out?"

"Ha. Bev promised to be there every minute, but soon she started leaving, 'for just a sec,' or sending her housekeeper, who constantly went outside to smoke, and some days the director lived in fear of a surprise state inspection. Can you imagine us losing our license?" She paused, shaking off the prospect. "Then, to make matters worse, Bev came in and organized the Friday morning Shabbat celebration into this whole big rigmarole, and she made all the other mothers participate."

"Are we talking more than challah, cream cheese, and apple juice?" Louise asked. "I mean, what can you do with a nursery school Shabbat? Those kids don't really understand that they are celebrating the Sabbath, which doesn't even start until sundown."

"Don't ask," Wally said. "They could barely sit still for

five minutes at that age. It was a real pain in the neck, and there she was, eight-and-a-half-months pregnant, and she's in this kitchen telling us how to cut the gefilte fish into geometric shapes to enhance learning." Wally checked to see if Beverly had moved into hearing range. "I was so glad when she decided another nursery school would be more prestigious."

A crash came from across the room. "I told you not to do it that way!" Bev said. Crimson-faced, Erin stepped over what she had dropped on the floor and went out of the kitchen. Toby, whose lime-green apron was streaked with food, ran after her, apologizing profusely.

"I'll clean it up," Marianne said. She pulled a wad of paper towels off the roll and, holding up her long dress, bent down to wipe up five cups of ricotta cheese.

"She wasn't straining the cheese right," Bev explained to the general audience. "The vegetable soufflé would be lumpy if she did it that way. I don't know why she had to be so sensitive."

Toby came back scowling. She spoke quietly to Bev, gesturing toward the door the whole time.

"I can't help how she feels," Bev said, not quietly at all. "Look, you know how it is with them. What did that old man once say about converts? You can't make a silk purse out of a sow's ear. Get it? A sow? A pig? Traif. Ha!" She laughed. "I get such a kick out of that one."

"Shh. She's right outside. She'll hear you." Toby started to go around the corner toward the ballroom through which Erin had gone. But then the sound of the far door slamming confirmed that she'd left.

And in all likelihood, thought Wally, Erin was not coming back.

Tad picked up the phone with a flourish. He was looking forward to this call—it would put him back where he should be, on top of the heap. No one had a better story than this, and it would cancel all his past debts. He practically chortled while he dialed that old familiar number.

"What d'ya want?" Tad's former editor, Bill Hart, growled.

Tad knew he sounded smug, but he didn't care. He was in the catbird seat and he knew it. "I've got a hundred million dollar story and I'm gonna let you beg me to give it to you."

"You think I'm gonna beg you for a story?" the editor said. "You, the idiot who cost this magazine ten million dollars?"

"Hey," Tad said. "You'll be ninety million ahead of the game with what I've got."

"Sure. That's what you've said before."

"This time is different. What I have is worth—"

"Seymour, you always have squat, and that's about what you're worth. Go peddle your liability suits elsewhere."

The clattering of the receiver just before the line was disconnected told Tad that Hart's aim at the phone cradle hadn't improved at all. Neither had his judgment. He was going to be sorry. Tad dialed his biggest competitor.

"Did Bill Hart set you up to try to get my butt sued off like his?" the man said. "Forget it."

He tried several tabloids on the next level down, lowering his asking price accordingly. He pitched the outlines of his story to some near the bottom of the barrel, but three hours later, another person said, "Do you have proof? I must have something in writing, even if it's only a statement from someone who would know. Who's your source?"

Tad wasn't about to reveal Bev Cohen to this guy or anyone else. But nothing other than a name would convince the editor.

Disappointed, Tad hung up the phone. The call had been no surprise. It was the same with every other editor he'd contacted. He was holding out for the big money on this one, and he knew he'd get it. But they wanted proof, and so far he didn't have much more than a hunch that he was right. That she was right. He wondered if he could somehow convince her to photocopy the file, to prove she knew what she was talking about. After all, she didn't know he was a tabloid reporter.

Chapter Three

By the time Wally got home, she was exhausted. They had made five pound cakes and seven lemon poppyseed loaves, because the synagogue's loaf pans turned out to be smaller than Wally was accustomed to. Working with Louise had been fun, but there had been a lot of tension with Beverly in the kitchen the whole time.

"You look tired," Nate said, as he reached out to hug her. "Mmm. And your hair smells like cake. Are we going to have any, or is this just for the temple?"

"Sorry. But you'll get to eat some of it on Sunday at the dinner."

Nate snuggled his face in her hair. "Mmmm. I can't wait. But maybe I can stay really close to you and pretend . . ."

Wally laughed at her husband. He was certainly more playful since their youngest child went off to college. But dinner would not make itself, and after all the food aromas, Wally was starved. Separating herself from her husband, but promising to return to his side later, she started dinner.

A few minutes later, Wally hit the remote, turning on the television news. "Oh, we're late. We missed the important headlines. I think we're up to the glitz."

File footage of a gala movie opening was being shown with a voice-over explanation by the station's entertainment reporter, Maggie Faulkner. "The stars will be out in our area again tonight as the newest Tom Cruise movie opens, continuing our Christmas movie season. It will no doubt be as glamorous as the last opening, which you see on your screen. We'll have film coverage and a wrap up at eleven." The image of a movie marquee with people in evening gowns underneath was replaced by the face of the local news anchor. "Thank you, Maggie," he said. Then, looking seriously into the camera, "Join us tonight, as we go undercover into the dark world of teenage runaways. Our cameras will reveal the realities of living on the street." He changed his face to a smiling one. "And we'll show you what some area residents are doing to ensure that some of our less fortunate neighbors will have a merry Christmas this year. Now, for our Jewish friends, Happy Chanukah."

Wally scowled as she put dinner on the table and turned off the television. "I went to the mall again yesterday," she said. "Don't roll your eyes like that, Mr. Mail Order. Besides, that isn't my point. You wouldn't believe what I saw. They had a giant menorah with Chanukah presents underneath."

"They're only trying to give equal time."

"You know how I feel about this. Chanukah isn't the Jewish Christmas. It just happens to fall at the same time of year. You should see all the trouble I have with the students in my class. I wish Chanukah happened in February or something."

Nate had the look of a man who didn't want to hear griping about that subject again. "Something funny happened today."

"You're changing the subject."

"You've got that right. Don't you want to know what it was?"

"Apparently not as much as you want to tell me."

Nate pretended to clam up.

"Okay," Wally said. "Tell me."

"I wrote three policies on houses in town that are scheduled to be used for filming that movie. They paid six times the yearly rate for the two months."

"How could you overcharge them like that? Do you think that just because it's a big budget Hollywood film you should price gouge?"

Nate scowled. "You should know me better than that."

"I thought I did."

"The producers insisted. I told them it wouldn't cost that much, but they assured me that this was for more than just damage."

"Are they planning to burn them down?"

"I don't think so. But if I were the owners, I'd be worried, even though the houses are getting complete makeovers."

"They are?"

"Yes. That's part of the deal. Not only do the owners get a huge fee, the houses are, at least cosmetically, made better. Maybe . . ."

The way Nate's voice trailed off had Wally wondering. "Maybe what?"

"I was just thinking. The set director was eyeing the barn. He said they couldn't use it for this movie, but that maybe someday it would come in handy. He made me promise not to tear it down without telling him." Nate shook his head. "Wouldn't it be strange if it was in some movie?"

"If they ever use it," Wally said, "get them to include the house too. I've always wanted a makeover."

The next afternoon in the synagogue kitchen, there was a certain solemnity over the group, since Erin's perky chatter was missing. A woman named Gail, wearing an Ohio State sweatshirt, tried to fill in wherever she could, but seemed to always be in Beverly's way. Since Louise was not scheduled to work that day, Gail offered to pitch in and help Wally with the sheet cakes.

Beverly, dressed in teal silk and taupe heels, sauntered over into the baking area. "Don't let her help you, hon," she said to Wally. "Her cakes always come out tasting like cardboard. That sugary frosting you're planning to use will never cover up the taste."

Gail left. Nancy was right behind her.

Wally had a brief fantasy of taking Beverly's skinny body and stuffing it down the drain in the sink. She shook off the image and turned to look for Toby, who nodded. Once she saw that Toby would support her, she gently took Beverly's hand and looked up, right into her sapphire blue-tinted contacts. "Don't trouble yourself with my area," she said, careful to keep the menacing tone out of her voice. "I can take care of it."

"Well, I was just trying to help," said Beverly, as she tried to pull her arm out of Wally's grasp. Her eyes widened when she found that difficult to accomplish. She seemed surprised that someone as small as Wally could be so strong.

Wally smiled. "And please don't insult anyone else with your kind words."

As Beverly slunk back into her own area, the people who were behind her silently applauded. Wally took a few bows, and went to find Gail and Nancy.

Nancy was in the parking lot, where Gail sat in her car, slumped over the steering wheel. Wally had her suspicions confirmed. Gail looked up at her, in tears. Nancy was teary-eyed too.

"I'm sorry," Gail said, as she rolled down her window. "I can't believe I'm crying like a little girl. But she just makes me so mad. She sounds like the girls I went to junior high school with."

"She acts like it too," Nancy said. "It practically gives me nightmares sometimes, how she is to people. And she knows how much her words hurt."

"She's totally obnoxious," Wally agreed. "But we're stuck with her. Listen, Gail, why don't you take today off, and come back tomorrow? I could use the help then too, and you can stay away from her. Hopefully, we won't have to work on another project with her until the next big dinner."

"I guess."

"And look at it this way. We're only going to be working until two tomorrow, so they can clean the kitchen for Shabbat. That won't be so bad. Just think about the serving committee having to deal with her on Sunday."

Gail bit her lip. "I'm on that committee too."

"The poor thing," Wally said, as Gail's car rolled out of the parking lot. Nancy just shook her head.

When Wally and Nancy returned to the kitchen, they found that the lack of lackeys didn't seem to faze Beverly. She still wielded a mighty wooden spoon. "Okay," she said, to the almost empty room, "I think we're in good shape. All we have to do now is get the rest of the salads done, and work on the platters." She looked around blankly. "What happened to my crew?"

Toby rolled her eyes. Since two other people had quit because of Beverly's tongue, Marianne was sweating over a huge bowl of yams by herself. She had a giant potato masher and she was struggling to flatten and mix the potatoes that they had boiled the day before. With each thrust of the masher, the hem of her long dress brushed on the floor. "Are you sure this is right, Beverly?"

Bev walked over to the counter at which Marianne stood. There were some bits of potatoes on the stainless steel counter top, and she took a fork and flicked them into the bowl. "I'm sure." She went back to working on the pasta salad.

Wally started making the cream cheese frosting for her sheet cakes.

"I didn't know you were planning to use cream cheese," Bev said as she wandered back into Wally's area. "That's a good idea."

Wally didn't point out that not only hadn't she asked, she knew very little about Wally's baking ability. Beverly was so arrogant, she simply assumed that no one was as good in the kitchen as she was. Well, Wally would put her brisket up against Beverly's any day.

Instead of responding, however, Wally just reached for

the orange extract. The chocolate cake would taste fabulous with the orange cream cheese frosting.

"How about taking a break?" Nancy suggested, after Wally put the frosting into the refrigerator to harden up a bit.

"Perfect timing," Wally said. "Where do you want to go?" She reached for her coat, grateful to escape the battleground.

Nancy picked up her own jacket and walked beside Wally to the lobby. "I thought we'd go to my house," she said.

She lived right down the street. Wally had been there on many occasions, ever since Nancy's son, Matt, was in her class in nursery school.

One of the time-honored traditions in Wally's classes was lunch with Wally for one student and his or her parent. Every child looked forward to it, as did Wally. In each case, the relationship between Wally and the student and family benefited, even when no strong bond formed.

Several of the lunches, however, turned into long-term friendships, such as the one Wally and Louise shared. Over the years, many of the students became almost like her own children.

In a way, it made Wally kind of sad, because now she had begun to be regarded more as a grandparent. But she filled that role with gusto. When Nancy's second child was due, Matt felt some jealousy, and Wally counseled his mother. After the baby was born, "special" time was available, because Wally offered to babysit for Matt's little sister. There were no relatives nearby at all, on either side of the Goldstein family, and Nancy and Wally became close.

A break at Nancy's house sounded fine to Wally. The Victorian house was one of the older ones in town, somewhat past its prime, with a slanted wooden porch that made Wally feel like she was walking uphill. Both women ignored it, engrossed as they were in the conversation about Matt's and Jenny's latest antics. A seven- and a four-year-old could get into a lot of trouble after school.

Nancy led the way into the large kitchen, which was early American in style. Four wall ovens flanked two full sets of burners beside enough counter space for several people to lie down. Every square inch of the room was immaculate. From previous visits Wally knew another refrigerator and freezer filled a corner of the basement playroom.

"How's your catering business?" Wally asked.

"Great. I hope. If I get that contract."

"What contract?"

Nancy's eyes sparkled. "I put a bid in on catering for the office park during the filming of that movie. They are afraid that with all the traffic, their people won't be able to get out, have lunch, and get back in a reasonable amount of time. I know it'll probably go to a bigger company, but I'd love to get it." She poured the coffee and put out a pitcher of milk, then opened a large tin. "Would you like a cookie?"

Wally reached in, selected, and tasted one. "Mmm. These raisin oatmeal cookies remind me of my grandmother's. She was a wonderful cook."

Nancy took a cookie for herself. "You are a great cook. I can't believe Bev had the nerve to insult you."

"I didn't let it get to me."

Nancy frowned. "It was pretty terrible what Bev said to Erin, don't you think? Why would she say a thing like that? It was as if she thought that Erin's conversion wasn't good enough."

"I wasn't aware that Bev was an expert," Wally said. "It isn't any of her business, anyway."

"Bev is so mean to everyone, and they are only there to help her," said Nancy, showing her own pain. "She criticizes and seems to know the emotional Achilles heel of each person. Then she zeros in for the kill. Did she have to make a nasty comment about Gail's baking? She only ever tasted one thing that Gail made, and it could have been an off day. Even if it wasn't, it was really cruel to say it in front of everyone."

Wally agreed. "I have a little girl in my class this year, a four-year-old, who reminds me of Bev. She walks around saying that she is wonderful, and has the best, although she calls it bestest, things. She tells the other children that she is better and her house is better, and, well, you know what I mean."

Nancy brushed away a tear and laughed. "A Bev in training. So what do you do about it?"

"It's hard," Wally said. "I try to talk to her mother about it, but she's kind of the same way. I can't tell this child that she's driving her friends away, but she is. But I haven't given up. She's young, there's still hope for her."

Nancy's mouth was set in a straight line. Sighing, she said, "I don't think there is any for Bev. But what happened between us is in the past. I have to look forward."

Wally checked her watch. "We'd better get back."

By the time they returned to the synagogue kitchen, Toby and Marianne had loaded all the potatoes into aluminum baking pans, covered them with foil, and baked them in the oven for the specified hour and a half. They were just taking them out when Wally hung her coat on the peg and went to check on her frosting.

As they opened the cover of the first pan of potatoes, a terrible odor wafted up and filled the entire kitchen. "What is that smell?" Wally asked.

"I don't know," Toby said. "I wish Beverly was here so we could ask her about this."

"I think it's nice that she isn't here," Marianne said. "This will wait until she gets back from her important appointment. She made such a big thing about it. I wonder what it was."

"Do you care?" Nancy asked.

Marianne shook her head.

"Maybe we should taste it," Toby said. She took a fork and put it into the potatoes. Then, after blowing on it to get it cool, she delicately sampled it. "Water!"

"You're kidding," Marianne said. "They couldn't be that

bad." She took a fork and tasted them too. "Oh, that's disgusting."

Nancy came toward them, sniffing the odor. "Can I ask, did you peel those potatoes before you mashed them?"

"No," Marianne said. "Beverly specifically said that we shouldn't. She read something about the flavor of the skin."

"I'll bet she did," Nancy said. "I read about it too, in the catering newsletter. But as I recall, it said that the flavor was incredibly bitter, that the potatoes could be baked in the skins to maintain moisture, but that the skins should not be eaten."

"Why didn't you say anything when we were mashing them?" Toby asked.

"I didn't really pay attention," Nancy said. "I'm sorry."

Marianne looked truly worried. "Now what are we going to do?"

"Let's just leave this for Beverly," Wally suggested. "What time did she say she'd be back?"

"About four-thirty," Toby said.

Wally resolved to be out of there by then.

The undercurrent of gossip that Tad Seymour was trying to peddle wasn't all that different from any other hot juicy uncorroborated tidbit of news, but there was a distinct possibility of a libel suit if every word was not true. While it wended its way from one rumormonger to another, each person resolved to stay away from it. By the end of the day, Tad still had not been successful in finding the proper place for his piece of dirt.

But as breezes blow, it brought the news that someone in the cast of *Stalking Sunrise* had something big to hide.

Chapter Four

The winds of rumor continued to blow, whispering behind closed doors, which all seemed to have someone holding a glass to his or her ear on the other side. Most people knew better than to let the producers of the film know that this gossip was flying around, because no one wanted to risk having the movie cancelled. They all knew that if it could happen to one movie, it could happen to another, and, as juicy as the rumor might be, it wasn't worth it. Nevertheless, the actors were aware that something was circulating, something possibly quite damaging.

Heath Maxwell flexed his former and future leading man muscles, threw a chair across his apartment, and watched with little satisfaction as it crashed into the wall and fell. There was only a minor crack in the plaster; he had been too far away to make a really big hole. For a second he looked around for another missile, but the ringing phone required him to put off the next launch.

He snatched up the portable receiver. "Hello," he growled impatiently, in his deep, cultivated baritone. This was no time for a disturbance.

"Hi, sweetie," said a syrupy starlet voice on the other end. "I miss you."

He groaned as he plopped himself down on the couch.

34

It was another one of them, and one whose voice he didn't readily recognize. He hoped there wouldn't be a guessing game involved. "I miss you too," he said, as neutrally as he could. It reminded him of a character he'd played who had been so emotionally empty that he could never show he cared. He wondered if she'd recognize it, and chastise him for not being happy she called. Whoever she was.

She did recognize the character. "Ooh, I just love it when you do him," she said. "He was so sexy."

This conversation was doing little to reveal her identity, and he really wanted to get back to raging about the injustice of his personal life being revealed in the tabloids and the devastation that would result. Not only would it be extremely embarrassing, it could also prove to be a career killer. He'd never have another chance.

But at the same time, he was kind of bored. "Are you busy tonight?" he asked. "I'd love to see you."

"Ooh," she cooed again. "I was hoping you'd say that. I can be over in a half-hour."

He could barely believe his luck. She would come to his place, and he wouldn't have to let her know that he had no idea who he was talking to. "Great. I'll be looking forward to it."

It was only after he hung up that he realized who it was. Ophelia. She was a famous enough model in her own right to have little need of showing off by having an actor pick her up. The only problem was that she was fond of a particularly nasty perfume and practically bathed in it. He needed to develop a sudden cold to keep her away. What the heck, he had been an Academy Award-winning actor, wasn't that why he would be the leading man in *Stalking Sunrise*? Achoo.

Melanie Jensen stretched luxuriously in the king-sized bed she shared with her husband, Tim, the most wonderful man in the world. A glance at the clock on her nightstand told her it would be time to get up soon, but she opted to stay where she was and let the children come find her.

Those darling children, whom she'd wanted for so long, were the joys of her life. She and Tim had it all—fame, fortune, love. But even without the money or fame, Melanie knew she would still be happy with her family.

The twins burst into her room giggling, and after trying to get on the bed and falling off, they managed to get up. They were fresh and sweet-smelling, since their diapers had already been changed by the nanny, who followed close behind them.

"Have my breakfast sent up," Melanie instructed the woman. "I might just spend the whole day in bed."

The nanny left and the twins jumped all over Melanie. "Where Daddy is?" one asked.

Melanie scooped him up and gave him a hug. "Daddy is working today." Reaching for her daughter, she brought both children close. "I'm going to miss you both so much when I make my movie. But Daddy will be here then, so you'll be okay."

When Melanie's breakfast arrived, she reluctantly let the nanny take the children away. "See you later, sweets," she called after the babies, with her heart full. She, who had never expected to feel this way, loved being a mother.

The ringing of the phone, and the news that a rumor was circulating about someone in the cast of the new movie, changed her mood. She was grumpy for the rest of the day.

Chapter Five

Kevin Cole knew it was impossible, but it was beginning to look as if someone remembered him. He'd been so scruffy all those years, and now with his clean-shaven preppy look, he was barely recognizable even to himself. He'd changed his name, simply forgotten those ten years, and just re-emerged from college. His mirror told him that he couldn't be any more than twenty-eight or -nine, thirty tops. Kevin was a young, up-and-coming actor, and he didn't want to lose that.

Ah, he had an idea. Maybe he should throw himself a little surprise birthday party. He could see the headlines now: KEVIN COLE'S 30TH BIRTHDAY BASH. That would lay the rumors to rest, and help him keep his role as the young drifter in *Stalking Sunrise*.

Of course he couldn't invite any of his old friends, most of whom were celebrating those embarrassing over-the-hill birthdays, the ones with a round number with a four in front of it. Nor could he invite his plastic surgeon, who had erased the squint lines from those years of driving a rig. He hoped everyone else would come. The rumors of a rumor about someone in the cast of *Stalking Sunrise* were weighing on his mind, and if it were about him and his ageless perfection, it was time to stop them. He'd pick a birth date and publicize the hell out of it. Kevin looked at his calendar watch. Nine-thirty on a bright Saturday morning. Time to get right on it.

Some observant Jews don't open their mail on Shabbat, but Wally usually did. It was nearly 1:30 by the time she got to it, because she and Nate had stayed at the synagogue after the service for quite some time to talk with their friends.

The first thing that caught her eye—amid the early Christmas cards, barely-on-time Chanukah cards, bills, advertisements, and solicitations for donations—was an invitation addressed in calligraphy.

She looked closely at the wording of the invitation, and considered the source. It was from Beverly Cohen, one of the least likely people to invite her to anything. The event, exact nature unknown since it was not billed as anything in particular, was to be held at the Cohen's house, which turned out to be, not unexpectedly, in the most expensive section of town.

The gold-embossed paper simply said:

Come and taste the joy of life with us on Sunday, January 21, at number seventeen, Whispers Lane, from 3 to 5 P.M.

Nate came over to see what Wally was looking at, and somehow managed to pry it out of her hand. "I can't understand this," she said. "Why would she invite us?"

The phone rang and Nate picked it up. Once he found out who it was, he laughed and handed the phone to Wally. "Louise is screeching something about calligraphy."

Wally took the phone. "Did you get one too?"

Louise howled. "You got one? I heard that a bunch of the parents of the Hebrew School kids got them yesterday."

Wally thought about that. "She must be having a big crowd."

"So let's go together."

"I wouldn't go to that. I'd never go to her house, just on general principle."

"What general principle is that?"

"That she is obnoxious. Besides, after the potato incident . . ." She watched as Nate, who was clearly trying to figure out the conversation from his wife's end, raised his eyebrows. Wally had to turn away or she would have burst out laughing at his puzzlement. "I'm not all that convinced she can cook."

"You should still go," Louise advised.

"But what would be the point? All I'd do is eat her food, and see her house, and avoid her like the plague. That doesn't exactly appeal to me."

"Oh, don't you want to spend the time with your friend?"

"Are you telling me that you are actually planning to go? Just to see her house?"

"That's only half of it," Louise said, giggling. "She also invited a lot of movie stars, from that new movie they're making in town, and I want to see them."

"What? Who told you that?"

"Miriam. She is one of Bev's close friends. I think they live next door to each other. Apparently Miriam knows about this party, because Bev had her in on the planning, but since she doesn't have an event that might require catering coming up, she isn't being invited. Not only that, she asked Miriam to watch her kids for the day. So Miriam is really mad."

"I don't blame her. It sounds as crummy as what she did to Nancy Goldstein when they broke up the partnership last year."

"Ooh, I remember. That was nasty. But get this. Nancy has agreed to help Bev that day. Go figure."

Wally's curiosity got the better of her as usual. "Okay, I'll be there. Now just exactly what does one wear to this thing?" She watched Nate roll his eyes, as she and Louise planned their ensembles. After all, there were famous people coming to this thing. One simply couldn't look shabby.

Chapter Six

Shariah Jones dressed as carefully for church as for a movie premiere and her many television appearances. All the while, she tried to ignore her stomach which was in knots over her upcoming nuptials. Today's service was one of the last ones she would attend as the minister's fiancée. In less than two months they'd be married and she would become the reverend's wife. Praise the Lord.

She checked the tiny scar on her eyebrow to make sure it did not show, then pulled lavender gloves over her long, pale-pink fingernails, and adjusted the brim of her lavender hat. Her outfit was entirely lavender, which was darker than the lilac suit she had worn last spring when the announcement of the engagement was made at the church. She adored all shades of purple, and wore it often. It set off the lovely, warm, milk-chocolate shade of her skin and also let her feel pure, righteous, and sober, the kind of woman who should marry Brother Wilfred.

Abstinence was quite often the subject of his sermons. To him, alcohol was the devil's brew. As soon as they met, he had asked her if she was an abstainer, stating emphatically that he would never be interested in a woman who had drunk evil spirits. He equated it with purity of soul and spirit. She had been a non-drinker for years and at the time she hadn't thought much about her answer, but once they

40

fell in love and he proposed, it had begun to weigh heavily on her mind.

She thought about her wedding gown, which was already hanging in her spare bedroom. It was of the snowiest white, with thousands of beads on the bodice below an illusion neckline that was both revealing and modest at the same time. The long full skirt blossomed from a wasp-waisted band of pearls, and the long flowing train extended from the skirt itself. It was everything she'd dreamed of as a child.

But there had been those rough college years, and that one terrible incident that she wanted to put out of her mind forever. Then she'd had her big break. In her desire to rise to the top of her profession, she hadn't had time to get involved in anything else. So, when she came home for a visit, and her mother took her to her church in Newark to hear the new reverend, she was reborn. No one in her family ever knew of her wild college days because she had been away.

In her mind and heart she was pure. She only hoped that Wilfred would continue to believe it. He was a good man and she loved him.

The auditorium of the synagogue had been transformed by the decorating committee. Metallic-colored balloons floated above every table, anchored by matching multihued ribbons. The lights were turned down, and candles softened the tone of the evening. People wore everything from gowns and tuxedos to sweaters with sequins and designer jeans. The mood was festive.

Wally, wearing a royal-blue, ultra-suede dress, and Nate, who refused to wear anything fancier than a sports jacket, tie, and slacks, found their friends at table eight. There were four couples in all, including their neighbors, Barbara and Jay Fine, the prosperous looking and well-attired Fisches, and Nancy Goldstein and husband, George.

Louise grabbed Wally's arm and steered her over to the hors d'oeuvres table. "I've already had a taste of everything there," she said, "but I'll go with you. Just one word of advice," she paused and looked around, "don't get too close to Beverly. She takes food right off people's plates."

"Why does she do that?"

"I don't know. But if she tries it again, I'm going to slap her hand. It's gross."

"Not that I'm advocating it," Wally said, "but why is it gross?"

Louise scowled. "Because she never gains an ounce. Maybe the calories stay with the person whose plate it is."

They were still pondering that when they returned to their table. Several teenagers came around and poured water into their glasses. The main course would be served buffet style after the speeches, but for now, everyone could sit and chat.

Wally had an opportunity to talk with Nancy without Beverly hovering around. "I heard that you were going to be helping Beverly with her big party. Have you made up?"

Nancy tilted her short-haired head. "Not exactly. She decided to pay me what she owed me for my half of the business, and she told me that right before she asked me to help her out. I was shocked by the sight of her check which, by the way, George, cleared the bank, so there." She paused after the aside to her husband, to catch her breath. "Now where was I?"

"You were explaining why you are going to work for Beverly," her husband said. "Especially after the way she accused you of having given someone food poisoning."

Nancy was pale. "I never . . . it was a simple case of stomach flu."

Her husband put his hand on her arm. "I know that. No one had food poisoning. That was my point. She used it as an excuse to take away your whole business."

"We got it straightened out," Nancy said in a meek voice. "Now I'm helping her with this party."

George seemed to be unable to get rid of his anger. "Am I to assume it is for nothing?"

"No!" Nancy swallowed. "No. She is paying me for that.

She knows that I'm in business myself and not willing to do the work for free."

"Did you hear anything about that contract for the office park catering while the movie is filming?" Wally asked, hoping to divert the conversation away from Beverly Cohen.

"Yes!" Nancy said. "I got it. It's perfect for me. I can provide it all and be home by the time Matt gets home from first grade. Since Jenny is in extended day at nursery school, I don't even need a sitter."

"On school vacation days," Wally said, "you can count on me, if you need someone to watch the children."

"Uh," Nancy said, "thanks."

"It's a nice second income for you," Barb said.

Nancy nodded, and looked over at George, who seemed a little pale, in Wally's opinion.

"Why do you suppose she asked for your help?" Louise asked.

Nancy's long earrings danced as she shook her head. "It's not clear, but I think she needs me to supervise the kitchen staff while she socializes. Anyway, I said yes, because I was in shock, and actually, she was kind of nice about it. She praised my work, and the whole schmear."

"So then you must know what this party is all about," Louise said. "And why we were invited."

"Why do you think you were invited?" Nancy asked, playfully.

Louise pushed her flamboyant red hair off her shoulder. "So that she could advertise herself to us. She wants to show off to all the people who might be having affairs soon."

"Is there something I should know?" Norman asked. "Does this mean I can have an affair too?"

Louise leaned over and pushed his shoulder. "Not that kind of affair. And why are you in such a hurry to find out if it's okay?"

"Stop it, you two," Barb said. She was laughing so hard

that tears streamed down her cheeks. "Nancy, please go on."

"You're right," Nancy said. "It's for advertisement. Beverly explained it to me. Wally, she figures that your Debbie will be getting married at some point and she'd like to cater the engagement party."

"Will Beverly pay for it?" Nate asked, looking hopeful.

"I don't think so," Nancy said. "She said that she sees a tent in your yard, and flowers and a dance floor."

"Call a doctor. She's seeing things," Wally said. "That isn't exactly our style."

"Is it imminent?" Barbara asked, breathlessly.

Wally considered Nate's warning stare. "I don't know."

"I thought you said that Debbie's been seeing that police detective, Elliot Levine, seriously," Louise said.

"Well, yes. I think they are serious. But it's still kind of soon." Wally had carefully avoided looking at Nate, but turned to him in self-defense. "I'm not pushing!"

"Oh," Louise said. "It would be so nice. He really is a terrific guy, and he won't be an underpaid cop forever. Doesn't he only have a few more months of law school?"

"I think he wants to stay in the law enforcement field," Nate said, "so he's likely to remain underpaid. But you're right, he is very nice."

Louise smirked. "And very good-looking. I wonder if he likes tents?"

The reference to Beverly's idea brought Nancy back into the conversation. "Whatever," she said. "And also, Bev knows that Chloe will be bat mitzvahed in a couple of years, so that's why Barb and all the other Hebrew School mothers were invited, and she figured that since Louise is in real estate, she could recommend her to newcomers who wanted to cater their housewarmings."

Louise chuckled. "Oh, really?"

Wally was dumbfounded. "That's so crass."

"That's typical of Bev," Louise said.

Nancy leaned forward and lowered her voice. "She invited several of the stars who will be in town shooting that new movie. She thinks she knows them since Doug examined them, and she hopes they'll use her to cater their affairs."

"More affairs," Norman said. "This is getting interesting."

Louise made a face. "Don't listen to him. But why would she think these people would come to her house?"

"Here's the best part," Nancy said. "She's having the party in January, because she thinks they'll have nothing else to do after all the holiday parties are over and before the actual filming begins, and so they'll come."

"So that's the logic behind the party?" Wally asked.

"That's logic?" Nate said.

Everyone laughed, just as the president of the temple, Ruth Hila, stood up and tapped the microphone. Hearing the laughter from table eight, she frowned, and squinted to see who was laughing at her. Louise picked up her napkin and waved.

Ruth smiled, relieved. "We have so many wonderful people to thank tonight for the lovely dinner they have prepared honoring our beloved rabbi.

"It seems only yesterday that he came to us, yet those years since then have been filled and made richer by him and his wonderful wife. We will have tributes to them later, during dessert. For now, before we call the tables to go up and partake of this delicious spread, we must thank Beverly Cohen"—she paused while people applauded—"and her crew, and Wally Morris"—she waited for more applause—"and her crew. Please everyone, take the time to look at the centerpiece cake that Louise Fisch has decorated in honor of this occasion. I'm sure it will be as delicious as it is lovely." Another round of applause was followed by people standing up and forming a line. Ruth's fervent pleas to do so in an orderly manner were drowned out and ignored.

By the time Wally got over to the serving tables, there was a big dent in the food. But a groundswell of people murmuring about latkes had begun.

Chapter Seven

The winds blew, swirled, and eddied, seeping into the cracks of the buildings of respectability, threatening the very foundation of truth, honor, and purity. Shariah Jones heard the rumors—something that could take a life and turn it around, something pertaining to someone in the cast of *Stalking Sunrise*. She couldn't bear the thought of being at the center of that rumor, because if she were, she'd lose the reverend for sure. If there were only a way to find the source, before it could be corroborated, maybe she could stop it. But how?

She prayed that the Lord would help her find a way.

The phone wires burned from Tad Seymour's endless efforts to get some corroboration of his information. But he was being stonewalled, and it was making him angry.

He turned on his radio and listened to the latest installment of the news from Hollywood. Another gala event was to take place in two days, the long awaited opening of a film that was sure to be a total bomb. As a book, the plot was stupid and the characterizations had been thin and muddled. But the author had sold the book to Hollywood before he'd even written an outline, and they'd had to make the movie, even though the book had been on the bestseller list only because of who wrote it. Millions of dollars were being flushed down the toilet on this one, in Tad's opinion.

He'd been trying to get his novel—which he was sure would be a bestseller—published. But so far he hadn't even been able to get an agent to represent him. Naturally he was using his real name, or as much of it as he was willing to reveal—H. Seltzer sounded okay, didn't it? Yet it was being treated like the trash he wrote as Tad.

Someday, he told himself. Someday he'd be considered a legitimate author. But until then, he had to sell this juiciest of stories, and he needed proof. With any luck, his little singing canary, Beverly Cohen, would be at the opening of *The Devil's Quarry*. Maybe he could get something concrete out of her then. It was worth seeing that piece of celluloid trash for that alone.

"In other news in our area," the radio voice said, "we go to the voice of Hollywood, Maggie Faulkner. I hear there are big doings planned for the Big Apple this week. Is that true, Maggie?"

The syrupy voice of Hollywood greeted her listeners. "Well, the long awaited opening of Skip Runyon's new movie, *The Devil's Quarry,* is scheduled for this Wednesday at the Starlight Theater. You'll remember that the leading man was axed weeks after shooting began when the producers discovered his drug problem, and they had to pay damages to another production company to get a release for the new star. Then there was a series of mishaps on the set, one of which was fatal to a stunt double. This flick ran several million dollars over budget and two months over schedule. If *The Devil's Quarry* doesn't capture huge audiences, Skip Runyon's days as one of the top new directors in Hollywood are numbered.

"But in the meantime he is getting ready to begin filming his new movie, *Stalking Sunrise,* starring an unprecedented number of former big names and up-and-coming stars. Unfortunately for Skip, there are already rumors flying about someone in the cast, something that is so huge there may be a potential for another big and very costly delay. I'm not teasing you folks, I don't know what the rumor is, but whatever it is, it is reported to be big with a capital B.

"In any case, rain or shine, all the stars will be out on Wednesday night for the opening. And we'll be there to bring you the latest from the world of Hollywood."

Wally switched off the radio in her car. Another gala event was about to take place, with movie stars and evening gowns. She was glad that she wouldn't be in a room with Beverly Cohen again this week, so she wouldn't have to listen to her talk about the famous people she met.

Kevin Cole popped open the cork on a vintage bottle of champagne and toasted himself in the mirror. The tabloids had covered his "thirtieth birthday" party with complete gullibility. What a bunch of idiots. Blowing a kiss at himself, and smiling as if accepting an Academy Award, he raised his glass in acknowledgement of his greatness. Then he frowned. There was another line on his face, meaning it was time to call his plastic surgeon. He picked up the phone. Maybe just a collagen peel, to look fresh. After all, his big movie break was imminent, in *Stalking Sunrise*.

Chapter Eight

Beverly Cohen's million-dollars-if-it's-a-penny house was entirely beige, both on its faux marble exterior and in its interior. The carpets, wallpaper, and furniture were all one color. Wally, not a fan of beige in any form, felt out of place wearing actual colors, even though her soft-pink cashmere dress felt like a warm mitten. Self-consciously, she tried to bend the uncooperative left side of her hair under. Her friend Barb, who could be best described as casual in a gray flannel skirt, black tights, and a red turtleneck, seemed to feel the same way. Louise seemed really uncomfortable, in a dark purple dress that set off her bright red hair. Naturally she didn't keep quiet about it.

"This place gives new definition to the term blah," Louise said. "Have you ever seen anything like it?"

Wally looked around for the three men they had arrived with, and found herself suddenly blinded by a flash. "What the—"

"She hired a photographer?" Louise squealed. "Oh, correction, she hired a photographer and a videographer. Smile, girls."

Barbara turned away from the cameras, and huddled close to Wally. "I can't believe it. Like I don't feel self-conscious enough."

"Talk about a spectacle," Louise said. "Where's Norman? Don't let him get near any sharp instruments—there's liable to be a murder."

They found that their husbands had left the main foyer and made a stop at the bar, where a uniformed bartender dispensed all kinds of alcohol and soft drinks. Each man held a glass, and gravitated toward the crowd in the dining room. That was also beige, with dozens of nearly colorless, potted paper-white narcissus bulbs flowering on the window sills. In contrast, the table, when they could catch a glimpse of it through the throng, was filled with brightly colored food which smelled absolutely fabulous. Wally immediately picked up a plate and waited for a chance to sample the cuisine.

The part of Beverly's kitchen that Wally could see through the swinging dining room door, as Nancy moved in and out replenishing the table, was also beige, a similar tone to the one on Nancy's already overworked countenance. Her face looked strained and Wally guessed that Bev was being her usual charming self.

"Hi," Nancy said, on one of her passes near Wally and her friends. "It's nice to see you."

Wally plucked a stuffed mushroom off Nancy's tray. "How is everything going?"

"Okay, I guess. Beverly only had two screaming fits. First she yelled at the photographers for coming into the kitchen. That's an absolute no-no, according to her. Then she fired the two waitresses. That means I'll have more to do." She grimaced. "But at least it's a paying job."

"Maybe she'll have to do it herself," Louise said. She paused, narrowing her eyes to gauge the situation, then added, "Nah."

The sound of an argument in the kitchen had everyone looking at the door. "I thought you told us she got rid of the help," Wally said.

"She isn't arguing with them," Nancy explained. "Erin Feldman is in there, and she's pretty steamed. I'd better go see if I can mediate."

"What do you suppose that's about?" Louise wondered out loud.

Barbara shrugged. "I don't know, but knowing Bev, Bev caused it."

Louise laughed. Suddenly she stopped smiling and looked at the archway to the hall.

Everyone turned to see who had just come into the room. It was none other than Heath Maxwell. He looked good in person, Wally thought with some surprise, noting his carefully coiffed yet somehow rugged appearance, and his riveting eyes. He was dressed in a manly, country-casual way, with a brown turtleneck under a tweed jacket.

"Where is my lovely hostess?" he boomed in a stage voice, sounding like all the waiters in New York who were too impressed with themselves to be believed to be making a career in culinary service. He was instantly bathed in the light from the videographer, whom Wally noticed had an assistant holding a high-wattage spotlight.

Flashes from the camera went off as Beverly stepped out of the kitchen and greeted him shyly, surprising Wally. Considering the blather she'd listened to about Beverly's exploits in mixing with the rich and famous, she would have thought Bev would be a lot more comfortable. It reassured Wally that things were more like she'd suspected, even though the last time she'd bumped into Beverly at the grocery store, she'd had to listen to Bev brag about all the people she saw at the movie opening.

Wally turned back toward her friends. "Close your mouth," she told Louise. "I can see your tonsils."

"I thought they were kidding," Louise confided. "I didn't think any of those people would really come."

"Well, then brace yourself," Wally said, assessing the new arrivals. She had no doubt about the identity of the lovely woman with the warm, milk-chocolate complexion who smiled at the group that gathered around her. It was easy to conclude that her tense companion, wearing a clerical collar, was her fiancé. Wally whispered, "Here comes Shariah Jones, and Reverend Wilfred. You'd think that she'd have more to do right now, with her wedding only a week away. Beverly can't be trying to get that job."

Louise nodded. "She's probably trying for a housewarming party, at least. But, if I may ask, how did you know Shariah is getting married next week? I didn't know you read the tabloids."

Wally felt she had to defend herself. "I had a haircut the other day and caught up on all my Hollywood gossip. Besides, her marriage is legitimate news, and it was in the people section of the newspaper."

"She really is gorgeous," Barb said. "And I think she's wearing the same shade of purple as you, Louise."

"Obviously a person of fine, discriminating taste." Louise scooped up a canapé, and popped it into her mouth. "Umm."

"This room is getting crowded," Barbara said, looking around. "Our husbands sure look happy."

The men were holding their own, as another wave of people removed their coats, handed them to the teenager Bev had arranged to check them, and headed toward the food. Wally smiled at Nate and his mounded plate as she and her friends moved into the living room to get out of the way.

The massive room they had come into was filled, like the dining room, with narcissus flowers that filled the air with an earthy odor. The large-scale beige furniture nearly overflowed with party guests. Barbara let out a soft squeak when she saw who was there. "That's Melanie Jensen and her husband, Tim Hawthorne," she whispered to Wally.

"Isn't that Kevin Cole?" Wally asked.

Louise's eyes widened. "He's so good-looking. I don't usually go for those younger stars, but he . . ." She raised her eyebrows suggestively.

Wally waved at Gail Herman and Toby Goldman. They were standing in a self-conscious knot pretending not to stare at stunning Melanie Jensen. But just then Jensen stood up, and, after tossing her magnificent chestnut mane, walked regally past them toward the dining room. All three of their heads turned simultaneously.

"What?" asked Marianne Sachs, who came into the room the way Jensen had departed. "What are you all staring at?" She squinted against the light of the cameraman and looked down toward the hem of her, as usual, floor-length dress, as if checking for spots. "Is my skirt tucked into my pantyhose or something?"

Toby went over to Marianne and apologized for herself and her friends. "We were just watching Melanie Jensen. Didn't you see her?"

"Is that who just went past me? Help me find a chair, I'm going to faint."

Gail took Marianne's hand and headed for the food. "You'll be fine, just stick with us."

Wally smiled and turned back to her own group. "Does anyone remember when Melanie was known as The Sylphid?"

Barbara thought for a second. "Was that her?"

"I remember," Louise said. "My son was so angry, because all the girls in his high school crowd went on diets to try to look like her. She had absolutely no shape at all, she was so thin. That was not what my son wanted girls to look like."

"Rachel went on a diet for a while," Wally said. "It was awful. I was on the point of worrying about her when The Sylphid stopped making movies and modeling and dropped out of sight. Her retirement probably cut the anorexia rate in the country in half."

"She's rounded out nicely," Louise said. "In fact she looks perfect. I imagine my son no longer hates her." Her eyes followed Jensen as she greeted the other movie stars and their hangers-on.

From what Wally had read in some magazines in the eye doctor's office, this movie would be a comeback for Jensen, who hadn't made a picture in several years. Rumor had it she was not all that happy that she'd been cast in the older woman role. But she didn't have a choice.

"She's wearing very unusual jewelry," Louise said. She had already commented that many Grosvenorians in the room seemed to be displaying their own jewels on this occasion. Diamonds, rubies, emeralds, and sapphires abounded. But Jensen was wearing ornate silver pieces, which Wally thought looked extremely attractive with her hair.

Wally especially liked the Celtic silver bracelet with the garnet in the center. "I think that it's very tasteful."

Louise just snorted. "I'm surprised Erin and the others all came," she said. "I would have thought they were too insulted to accept an invitation after what Beverly did to them when we were preparing the dinner for the rabbi.

"I talked to Marianne in the grocery store one day," Barbara said. "She mentioned that they were only coming because they heard about the movie stars from *Stalking Sunrise*. Melanie Jensen's husband is a hunk. This place is like heaven."

"Since when is heaven beige?" Louise asked. She lowered her voice. "Speaking of heaven, or at least someone closer to it than some of the other people here, Shariah Jones's fiancé looks edgy."

"Maybe because of the wedding," Barb suggested.

"Well, maybe," Louise said. "I've heard he's really sharp. I see Heath Maxwell also brought a date. That's funny."

"What?"

"He looks like he's about to sneeze. I'll be happy to get him a tissue."

"Behave yourself, Louise," Barbara giggled. "Ooh, who is this just coming in?"

"Where?" Wally strained to see who her neighbor was looking at, but all she saw was a woman standing alone in the hall. It occurred to her that while the woman seemed not to be a movie star, she didn't quite fit in as a suburban woman. She was too well dressed, too toned, and her hair too well cut. Most notably, she wore no wedding ring, the fourth finger of her well-manicured left hand being noticeably bare. And unlike all the Grosvenorians in the room who seemed to gravitate toward each other like magnetic marbles, the newcomer stood away from everyone, looking instead at someone else in the dining room.

"That's Janet Finkelman," Barbara said. "I think she is really close with Beverly, which might explain why she's here."

"What do you mean?" Wally asked.

"Well, she doesn't fit any of the other categories. She isn't a movie star who was examined by Doug, and she doesn't have any children even close to bar and bat mitzvah age. Unless she's engaged and Bev is trying to get her business for that." Barbara paused a minute, then shook her head. "But I don't think so. I heard that since her divorce, when she actually lost custody of her children," she paused again as every eyebrow in listening range went up, "she's been leading a quiet life in the city."

Louise snorted.

"That was unladylike," Barbara said. "Do you know something?"

"I shouldn't say."

"You can tell us," Wally prompted.

Louise looked around to see who was in earshot. Then she lowered her voice even more than it had been and leaned toward Wally and Barbara. "Norman told me that someone who came into the pharmacy mentioned that he saw Doug with Janet at a restaurant in New York."

Although the disclosure might have significant meaning, Wally knew there was an innocent possibility. "Nate sometimes has lunch with friends of mine, if he happens to have business near where they work."

"This source said that he was reasonably sure they were holding hands with each other under the tablecloth."

"How can you believe that?" Barbara asked innocently.

Wally shook her head. "You never know."

"Tell me," Louise said. "What did she do to lose her kids?"

"From what I heard," Barbara said, "it wasn't anything

like infidelity or bad parenting or the kids' preference. In fact, her husband is kind of on the cold, strict side. I've seen him with the children . . ."

"He lives in town?" Louise interrupted.

"No, I think they live in Livingston. I saw him with the children at Toys 'R' Us."

"I remember that place," Louise said. "I'm glad those days are over."

"I'm back in those days again," Wally reminded her.

"Yes, grandma, I forgot." Louise smiled. "I guess I won't mind when that happens to me. My kids should only be married and financially independent first." She crossed her fingers.

Louise was straying from the point and Wally nudged Barbara to go on.

"Well," she explained, "because I still have little ones who are invited to birthday parties on a weekly basis, I have to go. One day I saw Janet's husband, ex that is, and he was with their kids, telling them about a thousand times that he wasn't going to buy them anything because they weren't behaving. But they were!"

"So how did he get the kids?"

"She wanted to go to law school, and he had to pay, and she wanted to live in the city, and he wouldn't let the kids go live there. They were about three and five at the time, and Janet let them stay near their friends. She said it would be temporary, while she was in school, but when she graduated they were really entrenched, and she couldn't get them to make the change to Manhattan."

"What a shame," Wally said. "That must be so hard on her."

"She has visitation every weekend," Barbara said. "But she's here today, without her kids, so I guess she can handle the separation."

"So who is she staring at?" Wally asked.

"I can't see from here," Louise said. "Maybe one of the movie stars. Let's go back to the dining room and get some more food. This stuff isn't bad."

Nancy was still buzzing around when they got there. Her face was perspiring, and Wally could see she was gritting her teeth. But Nancy smiled when she saw the three of them.

"Erin isn't still in there fighting with Bev?" Wally asked. "I haven't seen her once."

"No," Nancy said. "She left an hour ago. She tried to get her husband to leave but he said he'd see her later. The food is too good. She said that if that was the case, he'd better stock up."

"What were they fighting about?" Barb asked.

"Apparently," Nancy whispered, "Bev's been blocking Erin's nomination as Sisterhood president."

"Oh."

Nancy shook her head. "What can I say? Some things never change. At least there is only another hour to go," she said. "Then there's clean-up of course . . ." Her smile faded. She rushed through the swinging door to the kitchen.

A moment later, she was back with another tray of canapés, looking annoyed. "She's in there giving everyone who walks through a tour, while I run around refilling platters. And she's doing that thing again."

Wally chose a tartlet from the tray. "What thing?"

"The thing where she takes food off people's plates. She does it every time someone comes near her. And you should see their faces. Their mouths open as wide as Bev's does when she pops their food into her mouth."

"Wally does that when she feeds her granddaughter," Louise said.

Nancy laughed. "That's not why. Their mouths fall open in shock at how weird Beverly is."

"Who's in there now?" Barb asked.

"Heath Maxwell. Five minutes ago it was Melanie Jensen. How am I supposed to function with that kind of pressure?"

Louise brought her hand to her forehead in a salute. "We who are likely to hear her brag about this for the next few years, thank you for the warning. We will avoid her at all costs."

Barbara giggled again. "This food isn't going to agree with me if I keep laughing while I'm eating it."

Wally finished what she was chewing and nodded. "I'm not going to feel like making dinner if I eat any more."

"What's good to eat here?" a male voice asked. Wally turned and saw Tim Hawthorne standing right next to Louise. He had a big smile on his face, and looked open, handsome, and human, in what had to be a $600 cashmere jacket and a Jerry Garcia tie. Louise looked green.

Hawthorne picked up a California roll, one that Wally had avoided because it looked like it had crab meat inside. "Mm," he said, when he finished it. "These are almost as good as my wife's." He looked around the room. "I wonder where she went," he said, before taking another canapé. Wally waited for Barbara or Louise, both of whom had practically drooled over the man, to say something. But the two of them just stood there struck dumb.

He continued speaking into the void. "Last week Melanie was going to send her regrets, but Wednesday night she decided we were coming." He smiled again, a truly charming smile. "I'm glad we did, with such lovely company."

Wally suggested that Hawthorne try some of the desserts, which had been brought out in the last half-hour. The two of them chatted about the food and his children for a bit, while Wally made every effort to have her friends join in. Nothing she said caused them to unseal their mouths. After a while, Hawthorne moved away, convinced, Wally was sure, that her silent friends were mutes.

"I think it's time for us to go," Louise said. "We have now proved that we are without brains."

Barbara went to the den to find her husband. Louise followed, with her head hung in shame.

Wally stopped them. "Wait a minute, ladies. If we're going, you can't forget your manners as well as your minds. We must thank our hostess before we leave."

They worked their way back through the crowd in the

dining room, and, after asking Nancy where Bev was, they pushed the swinging door into the quiet of the kitchen.

Beverly was there alone, fluttering back and forth between the ovens and her long counter.

"We have to leave now," Louise said, assuming the role of spokesperson for the group. Wally wondered where Ms. Spokesperson was a few minutes ago when she was left to talk to Tim Hawthorne by herself, but allowed Louise to proceed. "The food was delicious."

"We'll tell all our friends," Wally promised.

Beverly nodded happily, but to Wally's practiced mother's eyes, her flushed face looked feverish.

"Do you feel okay?" Wally asked.

"Isss warm in here, isn't it?" Bev asked, barely moving her lips.

"Not really," Barbara said. "But you don't look too well."

"Thansss a lot," Bev said, with a forced smile. "Really, I'm okay. I've jusss been sampling too much. It seems like everyone but you three has been in here feeding me. I haven't even had a chance to mingle outside with my guests." She pulled another tray of sorbet out of the freezer and closed the door. "But then again, since they've all been in here, I guess it doesn't really matter."

"You should try some ginger ale," Wally prescribed.

"Thansss," Bev said. "I will. And thansss for coming. I hope you enjoyed yourselves."

They went back through the dining room and, since most people had already left, had no trouble reaching their coats in the cavernous hall closet. It wasn't until they were nearly out the front door that Barb commented that Bev had actually sounded sincere, not bragging at all.

"She must really be sick," Louise concluded.

Chapter Nine

"**I** still can't believe this," Louise said, smoothing her black skirt. "It's positively chilling."

Barbara daubed at her eyes. "I can't believe it either. Beverly was so young. How could this happen?"

"Let's go inside," Wally said, gently pushing Barbara into the lounge of the funeral home, where the grieving widower sat with his family. "We must pay our respects."

"She was fine just two days ago," Barbara said. "She looked so good and . . ."

Louise was subdued, for once. "If you remember correctly, she looked ill when we saw her. I heard they took her to the hospital about an hour after the last guest left. They say she died just after eight."

"Was it an aneurysm or something?" Barbara asked. "How does a healthy person like that suddenly die?"

"I don't know," Louise said. "I got my information from Nancy and she didn't know anything other than about fifteen minutes after we left Bev ran up to her room to lie down because she was so sick. She was nearly comatose when Doug went to check on her later. He tried and tried to wake her, but he couldn't. Some doctor. He had her taken to the hospital where she died of respiratory and cardiac arrest."

"I heard someone say when we came in that the funeral

couldn't be until today because they did an autopsy," Wally whispered, as they moved closer to Doug. He sat on a chair in the visiting room of the funeral home and greeted each person as they came to tell him how sorry they were. Wally recognized many of the local people among the crowd of murmuring mourners.

Doug looked as pale as any human could look and still be alive. His red-rimmed eyes continually watered and he sat hunched and disbelieving as Toby Goldman whispered in his ear.

Wally felt awkward as she spoke to Doug. She mumbled, "I'm so sorry, she was such a beautiful woman, and she will be missed." He smiled as best he could, and Wally moved aside to let Barbara have a turn.

"Please come this way, everyone," the funeral director said. Wally followed her friends to the chapel. The men in attendance picked up black yarmulkes which were in a basket near the door and the women put black lace doilies onto their heads with the hairpins that were provided, before entering the chapel.

Beverly's coffin was the focal point of the room. It stood in front of a window which had a little grotto behind it, lending a peaceful outdoor feeling to the chapel. Wally and her friends found seats midway to the back, near several other women from the synagogue. They all murmured greetings, expressing their shock at what had happened.

The rabbi took his place at the podium and asked the congregation to stand as the family of the deceased was led in. His words, as he spoke of Beverly, were warm and very sad since he'd known her since she was a child. An older lady behind Wally sobbed, as did Beverly's children.

It took more than half an hour to get the funeral procession lined up to go to the cemetery. The cortege had to travel several exits down the Garden State Parkway and the sixteen cars driving thirty-miles-an-hour in the right lane further confused the already terrible New Jersey traffic.

The service at the cemetery was short. After the rabbi recited the twenty-third psalm, and everyone said kaddish, the prayer for the dead, the first shovelful of dirt was thrown into the grave. Many of the mourners took turns with the shovel, not stopping until the coffin was no longer visible. Wally choked back tears. The finality of the act and the faces of the little orphaned children were too much for her.

"Do you want to go back to her house?" Louise asked when they were back in the car. She started the engine of Norman's Cadillac, borrowed for the occasion since Louise's car sat only two, and waited for an opening in the stream of traffic filing past.

"I do," Barbara said softly. "Just for a while, okay?"

"It's fine with me," Wally assured her, from her place in the back seat.

Louise found an opportunity and pulled her car into the road. "Here we go."

The house was far more crowded than it had been on Sunday. Wally noticed that many of the people who had not gone out to the cemetery had come to Beverly's home.

"I think Beverly would be very upset to have missed this catering opportunity," Louise said. The dining room table was laden with food, cold cuts, breads and rolls, and several sliced turkeys, salads and pickles, plus the traditional hard-boiled eggs. "Although this isn't exactly her style, is it?"

Wally shook her head. She was about to make herself a sandwich when she spotted Elliot Levine among the mourners, looking very handsome in a navy suit, which accented his dark-blue eyes, and a somber tie. His light-brown curls lay respectably close to his head. Edging close to the young detective, she waited for him to finish talking to one of his mother's friends.

"Hello, Mrs. Morris," he said, turning in her direction.

Wally had to look all the way up to see his face, because he was so tall and she was so vertically challenged. "Hi. What are you doing here?"

"I just came to pay my respects," Elliot said.

"Oh, really? I didn't know that you knew Beverly."

Elliot was silent, and shifted his weight from one foot to the other.

"Her death was suspicious, wasn't it?" Wally whispered. "That's why you went to the funeral home and the cemetery too, right?"

"I really can't say right now."

"You know," Wally said, "I heard that Bev became sick soon after that party she had on Sunday, and never regained consciousness. We noticed that she looked a little ill right before we left that day. Do they think someone did this to her?" A thought jumped into her head. "Poison?"

The blue eyes stared at her in disbelief. "You were here?"

"Yes. A lot of us were. She had a party to show off her catering ability or something like that."

Elliot's eyes narrowed for a second. "I may have to ask you about it. We aren't sure yet, but if it turns out that it was poisoning, we'll need to question everyone who was at that party, and I'd like your observations."

Wally nodded solemnly.

"Did you know her well?"

"We weren't friendly, if that's what you mean. But I have known her for several years."

"Do you know of anyone who might have wanted to harm her?"

"Let me put it this way," Wally said, her voice hardly more than a whisper. "She made a lot of people angry. But I'm sure not enough to do something like . . ." Wally left the obvious unsaid.

"Don't worry about it right now. There is still a big question about how it happened. In the meantime," Elliot added, "it's important that this be between us."

"Absolutely. I'll let you get to work." She moved away, back toward where Louise and Barbara were talking to Nancy.

Louise looked at her watch. "I really need to get to the office. I have a client coming at two. She wants to see three houses this afternoon."

"Okay," Barbara said. Wally went to get their coats, and have another quick opportunity to talk to Elliot.

She found him coming out of the kitchen. "Call me when you need some information," she said.

"I will."

"Oh, and you should get hold of the video and photographs."

Elliot turned surprised eyes to her. "Pardon me?"

"Bev had people here, recording her party for posterity, the whole time."

"Great. Thanks!"

Tad Seymour could not believe his eyes. He reread the obituary three times, hoping each time that his mind was just playing tricks on him, and that it wasn't true. But by the last time he read it he was sure—the goose that laid the golden eggs was dead.

She should be happy, he thought, having her obit in *The New York Times*. Not too many people rated that, and he briefly wondered how it had been managed. But most frustrating of all, it didn't say what had caused her death.

"We've called the county, of course, and they are joining us on the case," said Captain Jaeger, while he cleaned his glasses. As he strained to look around, Elliot had an unpleasant view of the flabby bags under his eyes. "But you can be sure that we are going to keep our hand in on this one."

Elliot looked over at his partner, Dominique Scott, and winked. They had heard this before, concerning the case last year. The county took the case, and attempted to shut the police in Grosvenor out of the investigation. Elliot and Dominique, with the help of Wally Morris, had turned up most of the clues leading to the arrest of the perpetrator. Ultimately, Captain Jaeger had been commended for his department's work in solving those cases, which turned his usually sour temperament almost cheerful for an entire two days. He was after the same again.

"If you somehow manage to solve it and shut out the big guys," Jaeger said, "well, all the better." He put his glasses back on and did his imitation of a smile.

Dominique leaned across the desk to take the file that Jaeger handed her. Her long, slender, brown fingers flipped through the pages, and she looked over at Elliot. "It has been determined that she died of intentional poisoning, not accidental food poisoning, although in other circumstances it might have been considered a form of food poisoning."

"That was what we assumed since no one else reportedly got sick," Elliot said. "Do they know the actual poison?"

"They've isolated neurotoxin tetrodotoxin, which is found in the ovaries of a fugu."

"What's that?"

"It's a Japanese pufferfish," Dominique said. "I've heard about this. There are actually people who consider fugu to be a great delicacy. Sometimes they die because it isn't properly prepared. But it doesn't make sense," she added. "Fugu was not on the menu."

Jaeger turned back to Elliot. "What did you find out at the home?"

"Mrs. Cohen catered a party there that day. Several people in the community attended, including the mayor, as well as the stars on the movie they're filming here. They were patients of Dr. Cohen."

"We'll need a list," Jaeger said. "It would be good if we could find some reliable person to give us some inside information."

"Already taken care of," Elliot said.

Dominique turned and stared at him. "Who?"

"Mrs. Morris."

"She was there?"

"Yes."

A broad grin creased Dominique's model-gorgeous face. "Terrific."

Jaeger took off his glasses again, but this time he put them on his desk. "Is that the woman with the peculiar name? What was it? Balzacina? Proustette?"

Elliot was surprised that his boss remembered that. "Voltairine, after her great-aunt. But she calls herself Wally."

"She helped a lot last year, didn't she?"

That, in Elliot's opinion, was an understatement. Mrs. Morris had led them almost directly to the murderer. "Yes, sir."

Jaeger smiled, an almost scary gleeful smile. "Good."

Dominique stood up and headed for the door with the file. "Let's go."

Chapter Ten

"**I** appreciate your coming here so early," Elliot said as he handed Wally a cup of coffee. "I wanted to start with you to get an overview."

Although his desk was cluttered with papers, Wally could see a certain methodical order in their distribution. While she didn't want to delve too deeply into the psyche of her daughter's boyfriend, it made her feel that Elliot was probably a soulmate of Debbie's, and that was a good sign. "I hope that I can help," she said, after taking a sip from the Styrofoam cup into which Elliot had poured some incredibly stale coffee. She placed the cup on the desk with a firm promise to herself not to even consider a second sip, hoping her grimace didn't show.

Elliot handed her a printed sheet. "Here is the list of guests."

Wally glanced around, before taking a look at the page in front of her. "Where is Dominique this morning? I thought you'd be working on the case with her."

"She's interviewing some of the people who delivered food and beverages for the party, to see if any of them noticed anything. She'll also check the florist, because we were told that there were flowers all around the house."

Wally clapped her hand to her cheek. "Narcissus! They were everywhere, including the kitchen. I heard they're poisonous. You don't think that someone got Beverly to eat some of the bulbs do you?"

Elliot shook his head. "I don't see how, and she wasn't killed by that anyway."

"Oh. What was the poison?"

"Pufferfish glands. The poison in them was found in Mrs. Cohen, and in some canapés in the trash."

"Sushi?"

Elliot had been reading up on the subject. "Some sushi eaters think it's the fish among fish," he told Wally. "It's supposedly safe after the entrails are removed. If not, about sixty percent of the people who eat tainted fugu will die."

"Really? What does it do?"

The detective picked up a folder from his desk and opened it. "It says here that a person who has ingested that poison would have difficulty speaking and—"

"She did! Go on!"

"Then the victim would experience respiratory paralysis leading to death, although that could take a while, maybe even up to four hours."

"So," Wally said, "she would have had to have eaten it at the party, no earlier. But she didn't serve any fish like that. How do you think it got into her?"

"That's what we have to find out. Any ideas?"

"Well, I don't think anyone forced her to eat it, if that's what you think, or we'd have heard her yelling about it. Do you suppose it was an accident?"

"Unlikely. By the way, if she ate it, she wouldn't have known. As I understand it, you don't need to eat much of it to die from it. Just a few drops would do it. That's why we looked in the garbage for a small container, something that could have been used to carry the poison. But we didn't find anything like that there, or anywhere in the house, including in the narcissus pots you mentioned."

Wally put down the paper she had been studying, and thought for a minute. "She said something as we were leaving. Let me think about this."

She thought back to the kitchen, that beautiful, albeit beige room, and Beverly's flushed face. "That's it!"

"What?" Elliot's handsome face looked eager for information.

"Barbara Fine, whom you met last summer at our house, said that Beverly didn't look too well. I had noticed it too. Bev said that she thought she had overeaten because everyone but the three of us had been into the kitchen to visit and feed her, although knowing her, she was just helping herself to the food on their plates. She was speaking in a kind of slurred way, so it was a little hard to understand her. At the time I kind of took it as an insult, as if she was criticizing us for not helping her get food while she was cooking for her fabulous party."

Wally paused, and thought how nice it would be to have a real cup of coffee. It was so cold in the police station. "Don't worry," she continued, "none of us felt bad about it. If she hadn't fired some of her help in the morning, she wouldn't have been stuck in the kitchen working so hard. She was practically sweating buckets."

Elliot jumped up. "Maybe we've got the killer on tape, giving her food in the kitchen."

Wally shook her head. "I don't think so. The videographer had specific instructions not to tape in there. So did the photographer."

"Too bad. Tell me about the people whom she angered."

"I'm sure no one was angry enough to hurt her."

Elliot raised his eyebrows, reminding Wally that someone was angry enough to poison Bev. She swallowed hard.

"I hate to implicate anyone," Wally said. "It's just that I know some things about various people and Beverly. Of course there may be things I don't know about that are far more compelling as a motive. But here goes." She picked up the list, and stopped at the first person she knew anything about.

"Toby Goldman. I don't know of any particular motive she'd have for killing Beverly, but I do know of a good strong one she has for never asking her to help with a temple function again." Wally felt a strange chill, the kind her grandmother described as someone stepping on her grave. "I guess that's not an issue anymore.

"Then there's Gail Herman," she continued, "whose baking Beverly insulted. Do you think that's enough motive?"

"I don't know," Elliot said, making a note next to Gail's name. He put a small mark next to Toby's also, and Wally wondered if they were both suspects now because of her.

She looked warily at Elliot before continuing. "Marianne Sachs was insulted by Beverly about her children, but that's certainly not worth killing someone over, especially after several weeks of cooling off time. And the same goes for Erin Feldman, whom Beverly essentially called a sow's ear."

"I beg your pardon?"

"Well, you probably don't know this, but Mrs. Feldman is a convert to Judaism. Beverly implied that she wasn't Jewish enough. I think Erin was really hurt at the time, but she wouldn't have come to the party if she didn't get over it. Unless . . ."

"What?"

"She had a fight with Bev at the party. I didn't hear it, but I was told it was about Bev blocking Erin's nomination to the presidency of Sisterhood. Erin left early."

"Maybe she left after poisoning her," Elliot said.

"You can't really believe that, do you?"

Elliot shrugged. "Is that all?"

"Well, I guess so."

"Are you sure?"

This was serious business, Wally knew. She had no choice but to tell him.

"Nancy Goldstein's name isn't on the list," she said. "But she was working at the party. She used to be Beverly's partner, and there was a bad split between them, but I think it's been patched up financially. At least that's what Nancy told me."

"Maybe she was covering when she told you that," Elliot

said. "That, at least, should be a little easier to check out, because there will be a paper trail."

Wally hoped it was true. It was so strange to be talking about her friends and neighbors this way. They were all women she liked and respected.

By way of diversion, she said, "Aside from the movie people, there was another woman I didn't know. I heard something about her."

Elliot's eyebrows shot up. "Oh?"

"Her name is Janet Finkelman, and she is supposedly a friend of Bev's, but I heard that there may be something between her and Doug, Bev's husband. It's really just hearsay, but it may be worth checking out."

Wally watched as Elliot made a note next to Janet's name. "I guess if it's true, you'd have your motive," she said. "Or maybe Doug was the one . . ."

"We haven't eliminated anyone," Elliot said.

Wally sighed. "I wish I knew them better, so I could be of more help."

"You've been a lot of help, Mrs. Morris. If you think of anything else, please let me know."

Wally picked up her coat. "I'll be at the nursery school the rest of the morning. But I'm planning to be home this afternoon."

"Thanks. Dominique said to tell you thanks too. Even the captain was happy you were involved. He remembers you from last year, and how much you helped."

Wally blushed. "I'd love to help on this one too, in a purely amateur fashion, of course. I'll leave the professional stuff to you."

As she left she wondered if perhaps she'd laid that last comment on a bit thick. Oh well, it would be worth it if they did let her help.

The county assumed responsibility for the murder investigation, but worked closely with the local detectives assigned to the case. It was decided that each team would consist of one local representative and one county member, to cover all the bases.

Elliot's partner for the investigation, Inspector Davis from the Essex County Prosecutor's office, was of average height, with a lean, wiry build. He was also overly caffeinated, and positively jumpy sometimes. Dominique was paired with Davis's regular partner, a husky man named Brady, who was somewhat older than Davis but lower in rank.

At 9 A.M. Elliot met Inspector Davis outside the home of Dr. and the late Mrs. Cohen. Davis took a final drag on his cigarette and dropped it on the sidewalk. A moment later, though, he reached down and picked up the ground-out butt and slipped it into his overcoat pocket. Elliot rang the doorbell.

Doug Cohen was bleary-eyed as he opened the door. His mouth was taut. Two small children clung to his sides, both looking as if they had been crying recently. The younger child's nose needed serious wiping.

"Mr. Cohen," Davis said after identifying himself, "we're here to investigate the—"

He stopped, and glanced down at the children.

"That's doctor," Cohen said. "Please don't say anything just yet." He bent down and whispered to the children. They cried, and he stood up, looking stern. "Go upstairs now," he ordered. Turning back to the detectives, he said, "I'll be happy when they go back to school."

His tone annoyed Elliot. It was as if Cohen didn't understand that the kids had just lost their mother. He looked over at Davis to see if he had the same opinion.

Davis's face was unreadable. "Could we sit down?" he asked.

They were escorted into a small den off the main hallway. Dr. Cohen motioned them to sit, and sat too, in a wingback chair. "I have to apologize. I didn't mean to sound harsh, but I'm nearly at the end of my rope. This has been so horrible."

"You don't need to apologize," Elliot said. "At least not to us."

Cohen nodded. "You're right. I should talk to the children. They don't deserve my anger on top of everything else."

Elliot took out his notebook. "We'll try to be brief."

"But first, there are a lot of questions," Davis said gruffly. "Your wife is dead, and this is a murder investigation."

Swallowing hard, Cohen said he understood.

Davis asked some preliminary questions about what Doug Cohen saw, and who might have wanted to harm his late wife. He denied any possibility that his wife was not well liked. "She has so many friends," he said. "And she was always into all kinds of things. I never heard an unkind word about her."

Elliot thought Cohen must be deaf, or, perhaps, people didn't complain about his wife when he was around.

"Now," Davis said, "can you tell me how you think Mrs. Cohen ingested the poison?"

"Do you want my opinion as a doctor, or as her husband?"

"As her husband."

Cohen shivered. "Okay. We do not have fugu in the house, nor have we ever. I told Bev long ago that serving it was too dangerous."

"Did Mrs. Cohen want to use it?" Elliot asked. "It is not commonly used in the type of catering that I understood her to be doing."

"She had this idea once that she could cater a Japanese wedding," Cohen said. "I told her no."

"Did she always listen to you?"

Cohen let out a harsh chuckle. "Not usually. But in this case, I'm sure she did. It was soon after a case of possible food poisoning occurred with Bev's business."

Elliot hadn't had time to fill Davis in on that. He'd have to explain, but later. "Was that when she was in partnership with Nancy Goldstein?"

"Yes."

"So that was definitely food poisoning?"

"Er," Cohen said, shifting uncomfortably. "No, I don't think it was. But we didn't know that until later."

"Was that ever clarified?"

"No."

Davis cleared his throat. "I'd like to get back to the subject. Your wife made all the food for her party, isn't that correct?"

"She made it all. It took days."

"Mrs. Goldstein assisted at the party, didn't she?" Elliot asked.

Cohen turned his attention to Elliot's question. "Yes. But she only helped that day. She did not cook."

"But, even though the partnership was gone, Mrs. Goldstein was still in the business. Is it possible that she brought something for your wife to sample?"

Shock passed across Cohen's face. "Are you saying that she poisoned my wife?"

Davis glared at Elliot then turned back to Cohen. "This is very early in our investigation, and we're just fact finding. But would that have been possible?"

"I think so, but I thought Nancy came in empty-handed. All I saw her carrying was a uniform."

Davis pointed out that the tiny amount of the tasteless poison needed to do the job, only seven or eight drops, could easily have been concealed in a tiny container.

Cohen nodded. "Then anyone could have brought it in," he concluded.

The detectives agreed.

"Dr. Cohen," Elliot said. "I have heard that your wife had a habit of sampling food. Would you know anything about that?"

A flush rose up on Cohen's face. "I can't tell you how often I talked to her about that. It sometimes got so embarrassing, the way she took other people's food. But that doesn't explain how she got poisoned."

Unless it was in something on someone's plate and she

took it off and ate it, Elliot thought. But the crime was obviously premeditated, so how would someone know Beverly Cohen was inclined to do that? "Do you think other people noticed your wife's habit?" he asked.

The flush grew deeper. "Oh, yes. I think many people, at one time or another, have seen Bev swipe things they were planning to eat. Everyone in her family used to share the same plate at snack time. Whoever was quickest got the most." He grimaced.

Clearly, this had been a bone of contention.

"But it's absurd to think," Cohen said, "that someone could have been so angry about her habit that she was poisoned because of it."

Elliot agreed. "But someone may have been aware enough to set her up."

"Who?"

"That's what we have to find out." Elliot referred to his notebook for a moment. "Can you tell us about your relationship with your wife?"

"We've been married for twelve years. Since I got out of college. We married before I started med school."

Davis leaned forward. "That doesn't tell us how you got along. Had there been any trouble between you?"

"No, certainly not. I loved my wife."

Elliot had made several calls since his conversation with Mrs. Morris. Now he asked, "Do you also love Janet Finkelman?"

Sweat broke out on Cohen's forehead, and he sought to loosen his already open collar. He started to speak, but ended up sputtering and coughing so much that Elliot had to go to the kitchen and get him a glass of water. While the water ran, he took a quick look around.

The room was immaculate, completely different than he'd seen it during the immediate aftermath of the party and murder. A half-empty fruit basket sat alone on one of the vast expanses of counter space in the most expensive kitchen Elliot had ever seen.

Elliot tried to visualize Beverly sitting beside that

counter, preparing courses and chatting with her guests. Was she really eating off their plates? But how could someone have predicted that? Davis had cut off that line of questioning, but Elliot really wanted to know if Cohen was aware of anyone who was familiar with his wife's practice.

When he got back to the den with the water, Cohen took it gratefully. "So you know about the affair," he said, when he'd caught his breath.

"You don't refute it?"

Cohen shook his head. "After nearly choking to death trying to deny it, and failing miserably, what would be the point?"

"Some might think that an affair would be a motive for getting rid of your wife."

"Anyone who would think that would be wrong. I loved Bev, not Janet. I didn't do it. And I wasn't anywhere near Bev that afternoon. In fact, I make it a point to stay out of the kitchen, which is where Bev was all day, since I've learned not to get in her way when she is entertaining." His tone was bitter, and Elliot had the impression that the lesson was learned the hard way.

"Do you know who went into the kitchen?" Elliot asked.

"I think several people."

"Do you know which of them might also be familiar with Mrs. Cohen's habit of sharing?"

Cohen seemed to think about that for a long time. "I don't know about the people around here, from the synagogue and all, but her friends do, as well as the people who saw us at the benefit we went to. She made kind of a big scene."

"Sharing food?" Elliot found it hard to imagine a really big scene over her taking someone's hors d'oeuvre.

"Well, there was more to it."

"And which party guests were also at the benefit?"

Cohen gave the detectives a list. "Heath Maxwell, and Kevin Cole, and Shariah Jones, and Melanie Jensen. All of them, incidentally, were here with guests, but I don't know if those other people were also at the benefit."

Davis finished writing the names. "Do you have anything else to tell us?"

"I don't think so."

"We'll be in touch," Davis said, as he stood to leave. He waited until Cohen got up and walked them to the door.

"Please," Cohen said, putting his hand on Elliot's arm. He looked directly into Elliot's eyes. "Find out who took her away from us." Tears welled.

There was no doubting his sincerity, but Elliot felt he could have told them more. Once they were back on the sidewalk, he mentioned to Davis that Janet Finkelman was a friend of the victim's as far back as college.

"So she would know about that disgusting habit," Davis said.

"I guess she would. I'm going to move up her interview."

Chapter Eleven

Several calls to Janet Finkelman's office had resulted only in as many messages left. But at 11:15, her secretary told Elliot that she could be reached at the Cohen residence. He drove back over, after calling Davis to tell him where he'd be. Davis was busy at the lab, gathering the evidence for his boss. The county prosecutor required a specific format for the grand jury presentation.

Finkelman's car pulled into the driveway as Elliot turned the corner onto Whispers Lane. She got out, wearing a long cashmere coat, open despite the cold, with a business suit underneath. Shorter, heavier, and not as pretty as Beverly was, it was hard for Elliot to understand what Cohen would see in this woman.

Her high heels slipped on a patch of ice next to her car. Elliot was close enough to catch her arm and keep her from falling.

"Thanks," she said.

Her brown eyes met Elliot's and he could see her immediate dismissal as she assessed everything about him from his car to his overcoat. It was not nearly the quality of her designer coat, but he didn't earn what she supposedly earned. "You're welcome."

"Can I help you?" she asked, as if this were her home. "If you are a reporter, you'll have to leave."

"I'm not a reporter." He took out his badge. "I'm here to question you about Mrs. Cohen's murder."

He got some satisfaction when the smug look on her face disappeared. "That isn't possible right now," she said. "The family needs me. Leave a message at my office, and I'll call you for an appointment."

Elliot reached for her arm to stop her. "Ms. Finkelman, I'm sure as an attorney you understand what your obligation is. Would you like to talk out here or down at the station?"

She turned, and walked back toward her car. "I'll follow you."

When they pulled into the police station lot Dominique greeted them. She led Finkelman to the small conference room and made preliminary inquiries while Elliot got them all some coffee.

"I've known Bev since college," Finkelman was saying, when Elliot put the cup in front of her. "We were room-mates the first semester. We became instant friends."

"Did Mrs. Cohen know Doug Cohen then?" Elliot asked.

"No. He was my boyfriend's roommate and a really nice guy. I introduced them."

Elliot jotted that down, although there was little danger of him forgetting the look on her face when she made the statement. "Was his roommate Mr. Finkelman?"

"No. I didn't meet him until senior year."

"Did you ever think about dating Dr. Cohen yourself?" Dominique asked.

Finkelman's face reddened. "I . . . I never had any romantic interest in Doug."

Elliot flipped his book back a few pages. "I should tell you that we have information that would contradict that."

Finkelman turned her face toward him in what Elliot could only guess was an attempt to stare him down. That technique must have been useful to her, because it looked as if she had perfected it. It had no effect on him, especially when he placed a faxed copy of a hotel bill in front of her.

Her mouth, which had opened in what he supposed was

protest, closed again, and her shoulders sagged. "I guess we should have been more careful." She sniffled.

Dominique handed her a tissue. "Did Mrs. Cohen know?"

"I don't think so. We would all have heard the screaming. As much as she claimed to be my best friend, she wasn't the sharing type. Not that I would have expected her to share her husband, but she didn't share any of her good fortune. She wasn't even much help when I went through my divorce." Janet's voice had turned distinctly venomous.

"Did you hate her?" Elliot asked.

"You mean, did I hate her enough and want her husband enough to want to kill her?" Finkelman wiped her eyes. "Sometimes. But I didn't do it." She shook her head. "I loved her too. She was like a sister to me—a prettier, thinner, taller, and more successful sister. I wanted a piece of what she had, but I didn't want her dead."

By the time she left the police station, after Elliot and Dominique had finished getting her statement, she had regained some of her earlier air of superiority. But it left Elliot wondering if she'd been honest.

Dominique wondered aloud, along similar lines. "She actually admitted that she had a thing with her best friend's husband, and felt no remorse. She justified it by saying she was jealous."

"As if that were a valid excuse," Elliot agreed. "And if she so easily explains away luring her friend's husband astray, is it possible she gave herself permission to kill Beverly too?"

Dominique scowled. "Tell me about your interview with the husband."

"He is really hurting," Elliot said. "He loved his wife, even though he admitted how he behaved with her best friend."

"Did he do that so we couldn't find out about it later, and suppose that if he was hiding that, he was also hiding the truth—that he murdered his wife?"

"No, it was more like his conscience gave him away. The minute it was brought up, he started to choke." Elliot voiced his concern over what he considered an inconsistency. "From what I've heard about Beverly, I can't see why she put up with him. He is such a nebbish."

"That means a nothing, right? Maybe that was a good thing, for her. Maybe she liked being in control, and a strong man didn't suit her needs." Dominique shrugged. "Who knows? Why are you sneering?"

"Was I? I guess I was just thinking about his face when we questioned him about Nancy Goldstein, and how she lost her half of the catering business. He seemed more uncomfortable when we asked about his not letting her know right away that it wasn't food poisoning that made that person sick, than he did when we asked about how his wife might have been poisoned."

"Why didn't he tell her immediately?"

"His wife probably wouldn't let him. She didn't want him to tell Nancy the good news until she got what she wanted—the other half of the business."

"Did he talk about Beverly's habit of filching other people's food?"

Elliot nodded. "He seemed to know all about it. And to have been embarrassed by it."

He looked at his watch and realized he had no time left before he had to meet Davis at the home of George and Nancy Goldstein. They were going to take her statement there, since, as in Cohen's situation, there were small children to consider. Elliot rushed over.

Davis stood outside, impatiently smoking a cigarette. The sidewalk at his feet showed that he'd been there for several cigarettes and that he didn't regard this neighborhood as highly as the one where the Cohens resided.

Nancy invited the detectives into her kitchen, while her husband ushered the children upstairs.

"I understand you were in partnership with Mrs. Cohen at one time," Elliot said.

Nancy frowned. "Yes," she answered, slowly. "But we dissolved it."

Inspector Davis drummed his fingers on the table. "Was it because of the food poisoning scare?"

"That was what Bev said we had to do."

Her statement, or at least the way she made it, puzzled Elliot. Mrs. Morris had spoken highly of Nancy Goldstein, but she couldn't have meant this meek person who subjugated herself to a bully. "Did you seek advice on your own?" he asked.

"Keep your law school stuff out of this," Davis grumbled quietly so only Elliot could hear. "Mrs. Goldstein, why were you at the Cohen party?"

"Because Bev was paying me, and had paid me back for my share of the old partnership. I needed the money."

"Your husband's job isn't enough?" Davis asked.

Elliot had heard Davis's views on working mothers several times since the two of them met. It wasn't a progressive opinion.

"My husband's job was downsized at the beginning of December. I need every job I can get until he finds something."

Elliot was surprised to hear that. "I heard you were awarded the contract to cater for the office park while the town is tied up with the new movie."

Nancy Goldstein burst into tears. "I was," she sobbed, "but I lost it."

Several minutes passed before she could speak again. Elliot brought her water, and a box of tissues from the counter.

"I'm sorry," she said, finally. "I had such high hopes. It was almost a good thing that George would be home to help me. But all my dreams are gone. I have to start over . . . again. It's very hard."

"I'm sorry," Elliot said. In an effort to soothe her, he added, "Mrs. Morris speaks very highly of your cooking."

Nancy smiled.

"It's our understanding," Elliot continued, "that Mrs. Cohen spent most of the time during the party in the kitchen because she was shorthanded. It seems odd that she didn't have enough serving staff."

"She fired them five minutes after they walked in."

"Why?"

"They came in dressed for hot Saturday night dates— Bev's words, not mine—and didn't have uniforms. Bev thought they'd make the wrong kind of impression."

"Why didn't she just let them help in the kitchen if that was the case?"

"Because it was clear they didn't know what they were doing. The first one started working without washing her hands, and the second one sat down at the kitchen table, lit a cigarette, which, to my knowledge no one has ever done in that house, and asked Bev to get her a soda. I guess Bev thought she'd be better off without help like that."

"Since you were near Mrs. Cohen for a good part of the party," Elliot said, "we're hoping you were in a position to see who had an opportunity to put poison on Mrs. Cohen's food."

"I didn't see anyone with any containers," Nancy said.

Davis shook his head. "It could have been very small. A pillbox would have been plenty big enough."

"Really?"

"About seven drops, ma'am. That's all you'd need."

"Did you ever serve fugu?" Elliot asked.

"No. I don't get fancy. I once served blowfish from Florida to a group, but ever since I heard that even those can sometimes be dangerous, I vowed not to do it again." She paused. "Those can be purchased locally, you know. Are you sure that isn't what it was?"

Elliot had read about that too. "It was Japanese. A different toxin."

"Oh."

"Are you saying it's possible that Mrs. Cohen served that at the party?"

"No. I didn't mean that. It just doesn't make sense. Most people can't just go out and buy fugu. And certainly they can't just serve it to people. You need a license."

"So you're saying no one can get it?"

"Not exactly. It may be possible. Bev wanted to serve it once, since I had taken a Japanese cooking course and could clean it properly, but we never did it. That was right around the time we split up."

"So you'd know how to get at the poison," Davis said.

All the color drained from the young woman's face. "No! I don't . . . I didn't . . ." She closed her mouth.

Elliot wanted more information, and he thought that if Nancy burst into tears again they'd never get it. "We're not saying that we think you did it," he said, softly. "What we really need to know is who you saw near enough to do it."

Her breathing slowed a bit, almost back to normal. "I saw just about all the guests at one time or another, since I was also out serving. And most people came in to say hi to Bev."

She gave a list, which included all the people that Mrs. Morris mentioned, and all the actors in the new movie. "I can't figure out how any one of them could poison her, though."

"Did you see anyone put food into Mrs. Cohen's mouth?" Davis asked gruffly.

"What? Who would do that?"

"I have heard that Mrs. Cohen herself claimed that people shared their food with her," Elliot said.

Nancy shook her head, half closing her eyes while she did it, and chuckled. "Bev. You had to know her. People didn't share with her, at least not on purpose. She took food off any plate within ten feet." She stared wide-eyed at Elliot. "Don't tell me you haven't heard about that."

"Actually, I did." He didn't add that it was probably why someone was able to poison her. All the murderer would have had to do was poison the food on his or her own plate, and wait for Bev to grab it.

Nancy furrowed her brows. "Are you going to be able to find out who killed her?"

Davis didn't hesitate. "Yes, ma'am."

Tad Seymour finally got another cup of coffee when the waitress who was serving him deigned to notice his gesture. She had been leaning against the counter, smoking a cigarette, for several minutes as he tried to get her attention. As if it weren't bad enough that this restaurant allowed smoking, the waitress had to savor every millimeter of her cigarette down to the filter before stubbing it out.

"Can I get you anything else?" she asked, indifferently.

"What kind of pie have you got?"

"Apple, blueberry, coconut cream, tapioca pudding, and Jell-O," she rattled off, seemingly unable to stop her dessert recital at the end of the list of pies.

"I'll have some of the apple," Tad said. "And keep the coffee coming."

He should have sat at the counter, he decided, but he had chosen this seat because it faced the door. This was a very small restaurant, not like the ever-present Greek diners which dotted New Jersey's roads, although it did serve the customary Greek salad as one of its blue-plate specials. The cigarette-sucking waitress who came with his table was just bad luck. He had a very good view of the whole room.

He chuckled. Here he was in Grosvenor, pronounced by the locals as Gross Vennor. What a joke. A little suburban town trying to pretend it was real. New York, now that was real. He never felt really alive unless he was in Manhattan.

Speaking of alive, he wasn't making much progress in his research into the suspicious death of his golden goose. He had bought one of the clerks in the police station a big dinner the night before, but she didn't give him anything he could use in the way of information. She didn't even confirm whether it was a murder.

He couldn't get over it. He'd had to give up his plans for cashing in big time on his rumor because now that the big mouth was dead he couldn't make his case for having a reliable source. He surely could not get documentation now, and he had nothing to show for it. Yet, in his heart, he felt that Beverly Cohen's death and the person who caused it were linked to that rumor. That could be even bigger than the original story. If he had to stay in this backwater town for a year, he'd find out. With any luck, he'd turn it into a goldmine.

"Thanks for meeting me here," Louise said, settling into a booth. "I had to take a late lunch today. I'll bet you're really hungry."

"I nibbled while Nate ate his lunch," Wally admitted. "He sends his love."

"He didn't by any chance carry the policy on her, did he?"

"You mean Beverly?" Wally looked at her suspiciously. "You want to know who her beneficiary is, don't you?"

"Yes."

"He didn't write one for her personally, but he did write one for the business that she and Nancy had. You can't possibly think that was the reason for killing her."

"So it's definitely murder," Louise said breathlessly. "I thought it might be, but . . ."

"Elliot told me, but he doesn't want me to talk about it too much."

"How convenient to have a police officer in the family."

Wally shook her head. "A, he isn't in the family and B, he's only going to be a police officer until he finishes law school. I guess."

"He and Debbie do make a nice couple, though," Louise said. "I saw them one night in the city."

"Another sighting of a romantic liaison."

"Huh?"

"Oh, I was just thinking about what you said about Janet Finkelman and Doug. Do you think it's true?"

Louise let out a low whistle. "That could mean . . ."

Wally nodded. Neither of them would finish that sentence. "I had to tell Elliot what I knew about the people who were at the party. I don't think it helped. It couldn't have been any of us."

"Our friends don't do that sort of thing," Louise agreed. "Will Elliot be talking to all of us?"

"I guess so. He has to talk to everyone who was at the party on Sunday. After all, that was the last time she was seen healthy and alive." Wally looked around. "Are you ready to order?"

"We don't even have menus yet."

"I know what I want. Can you see where the waitress is?"

In the booth behind them, Tad Seymour could see where the waitress was. She was sucking on another cigarette. But he didn't care if she took all day to get their order. He wanted to hear what the ladies behind him—the little one and the bigger, red-headed one—had to say. Then, when they left, he'd go call the newspapers and television stations. It would stir up a whole lot more information if they were onto the murder of Beverly Cohen. If there was one thing he was sure of, there was no money in an unidentified murder suspect. But there were big bucks to be made during a sensational murder trial. What he needed now was information. And he intended to get it.

The local anchor of the six o'clock news turned his eyes to the camera and fixed a serious look on his face, slightly different from the sad one he'd used to tell a previous story.

"In other news in our area," he said, "police have just confirmed that yesterday, in Grosvenor, New Jersey, a town that saw a murder and a kidnapping only last year, a woman was buried, believed to be the victim of intentional poisoning. Details are sketchy at this hour, but an investigation into this bizarre murder has begun. We'll go live now to B.J. Waters, our correspondent at the scene, for this exclusive report that you will not see anywhere else."

A caption stating that this was live hovered above the reporter's head, showing a night view of a building. "Thanks John. I'm reporting to you live tonight from Grosvenor, New Jersey. I'm standing in front of the police station where an investigation has commenced into the death of Beverly Cohen, a young mother and prominent businesswoman in this community. Police aren't saying, but it seems there is a very long list of suspects, because Mrs. Cohen died only hours after throwing a gala party at her home."

"Earlier" was flashed across the screen that scanned the home and neighborhood of Beverly and Douglas Cohen, in daylight. "Dr. Douglas Cohen lives here, on Whispers Lane, in Grosvenor, New Jersey," said a pre-recorded voice-over. "His life was shattered on Sunday when after a party at their home, Beverly Cohen, his wife, just thirty-four years old, fell ill and died."

The picture flashed back to "Live" and the reporter at the station. "Toxicology reports have not yet been released, but police say they do not believe that Mrs. Cohen could have ingested the poison accidentally. We'll bring you any developments in this case as soon as we have them. This is B.J. Waters, in Grosvenor, New Jersey. Back to you, John."

Wally groaned and turned off the TV. The news was out. They were in for another media siege.

Chapter Twelve

Elliot was apprehensive about the Health Maxwell interview. He had seen many photographs of him, especially those in the men's cologne ads that seemed to be built around Maxwell. Nearly every magazine had at least one picture of him on a prominent page.

From what he understood, Viceroy, the cologne company, was also a major backer of the new movie, which led Elliot to wonder if that was why Maxwell, who had been less popular in recent years, had been given the lead.

He looked around the room. There were bottles of the cologne on the server in the dining room and several blow-ups of some of the advertisements hung on the wall. Elliot had studied the actor in the video which was made during that fateful party, but the in-person presence was larger than life. The actor sat in a splendidly casual, self-assured manner on a white leather couch in his enormous New York apartment overlooking Central Park. Elliot couldn't shake the feeling that the man was only acting relaxed, but he attributed that to the nature of the conversation. This wasn't exactly a social visit.

"Can you tell me how long you've known the victim?" asked Elliot's partner, Inspector Davis.

"I really didn't know her," Maxwell said, in an actor's

powerful voice. "I never met her before Sunday. I knew her husband. The doctor."

"Your doctor?"

"Not exactly. I saw him when I was examined for the insurance policy for *Stalking Sunrise*."

"Is that the only time?"

"Yes. Er, no. He has examined me for the same purpose before."

Davis looked at him, as if waiting for more. When nothing else came, he continued, "And you became friends?"

"No. It was a professional relationship."

"Then why do you suppose you were invited to Dr. Cohen's home?"

Maxwell rubbed his knuckles. "I just assumed it was a get-together. The movie is slated to be filmed in their town, and I understood the Cohens to be rather prominent there."

"Do you often go to that type of thing?"

"To tell you the truth," Maxwell said, in a condescending tone, "I had nothing better to do that day."

Davis was unperturbed by the flippant response. "Did you talk to Mrs. Cohen at the party?"

"Only for a few minutes, other than when I first arrived. I think I stopped in to visit her in the kitchen. She had been so insistent that I see it when I greeted her. I wasn't going to, since I have little interest in domestic activities, and I assumed she would come out for a chat, but she seemed to be in there nearly the whole time the party was on."

"Did you happen to see her taste anything?" Elliot asked. Ignoring Davis's look of surprise, he concentrated on the actor's face.

Maxwell gave a great act of thinking about the question. "Well," he said, thoughtfully, "let me think. We were in the kitchen, and one might expect that she would eat things in there. Yes, yes, I think she did."

"Could you say what it was she tasted?" Davis asked.

"Not really. I think she took something off my plate and nibbled on it."

Davis leaned forward. "Do you have any idea why she did that? Wasn't there other food she could have eaten?"

Maxwell tilted his head back, which gave the effect of him sticking his nose into the air. "Who can say?" he said dramatically, with a touch of fatigue, flicking his wrist and unfolding his fingers to reveal an open palm. "So many people want to touch things that I have touched. Perhaps it was that way with Mrs. Cohen." As an afterthought, he lowered his eyes and added, "Poor unfortunate woman. I wish there was more I could do to help."

"I need to ask you about the woman with whom you attended the party," Davis said. "We don't have her name, and we'd like to be able to ask her some questions."

"Oh, what a pity," Maxwell said. "She just left. Can I have her call you?"

"Her name?"

"Emma Quaff. I have her number right here." After majestically striding over to his desk, he took out a black phone book from the top drawer and wrote down the number. Davis took it from him and put it into his notebook.

"I think that's all we need for today, Mr. Maxwell," he said. "I'd like you to be available for any other questions that might come up."

" 'Are you saying I shouldn't leave town?' "

Davis chuckled. "You already left the town the incident occurred in. No, you are free to travel, but I'd like to have a number where you can be reached. Your agent's name should be sufficient."

Maxwell didn't need his phone book to write that down. He dashed it off and handed another slip of paper to Davis. "I hope I was helpful," he said. "This is such an ugly business."

Davis said nothing to Elliot on the way down in the elevator. But once they were outside, Davis threw Elliot the car keys and said, "Why did you ask that question, particularly the way you did? We know she was poisoned, but you don't expect someone to admit giving it to her, do you?"

"No," Elliot said, as he pulled out of the parking spot. "One of the guests I spoke to said that Mrs. Cohen mentioned that everyone but three of them had fed her. I wondered if it was true, but figured that wasn't the way to ask it. Tasting seemed like the kind of thing a caterer might do, and less likely to send up alarms in someone being questioned."

"That's true," Davis said. He opened his notebook and picked up the car phone.

When he was done, he shook his head, indicating to Elliot that he'd had no luck finding the Quaff woman. "Her machine was on," he said, "saying that she'd be away for a week in Texas, and to call her agent if there was a part available. I called his office and left a message for him to call back."

It had seemed to Elliot that Maxwell said that his companion had just been in the apartment. "I wonder when she left."

"We'll see," Davis said. He chuckled.

"What's so funny?"

" 'Are you saying I shouldn't leave town?' " Davis mimicked. "Does he think this is some kind of movie?"

Elliot shrugged and concentrated on his driving. They traveled back to New Jersey, to a beautiful old section of Newark, with large houses on tree-lined streets. Brady and Dominique had asked them to meet there, since there were no other interviews scheduled for that day.

The four of them were invited into a stately old house that Shariah Jones had purchased for her mother. The young actress mentioned that she would be moving out soon, since she was about to be married. Elliot saw a huge diamond on her finger as she waved her hands expressively, indicating that they should be seated.

The wedding was only a few days away, and Jones seemed to be in a hurry to get the interview over.

Since Davis was the senior man, he did the questioning. "How did you know Mrs. Cohen?" he asked, in a manner different from the one he used on Heath Maxwell. Now he was slightly fatherly and, although the young woman he was interviewing was gorgeous, Elliot noticed that Davis did not stare.

"I didn't," Jones said. "I don't even know why she invited me. I only saw her husband, the doctor, one time for an insurance checkup."

"Did you talk to her at the party?"

"Just once, as I was leaving. We went in to say goodbye to our hostess."

"We?"

"My fiancé and I."

"We'll need to talk to him."

"I'll give you his number. Is that all?" She half stood up, but lowered herself back down when she saw Davis's upraised hand.

"I have one more question," Davis said. "Did you see Mrs. Cohen taste anything?"

Jones paused in puzzlement.

"Let me think. I think she did. I think she ate something off my plate, if I remember correctly. I was still holding it when we went to say good-bye. I don't know why she did that though. It was so odd."

"Did you say anything about it?"

"I didn't, but she told me that she wanted to be sure that I had selected the very best of her canapés. I would have thought she could tell by looking though, wouldn't you?"

"I don't know, Ms. Jones," Davis said. "Well, I think I have asked all my questions. Please keep us advised of your location."

"My honeymoon plans are secret," Jones said indignantly, rising once again. "But my agent will know how to reach me if it is necessary."

The three male detectives were already standing, but Dominique was lost in thought. She cleared her throat. "Ms. Jones?"

The actress looked at Dominique with a liquid-brown gaze. She smiled, showing a perfect set of white teeth. It occurred to Elliot that her manner became more friendly when she turned to Dominique. "Yes?"

"If you didn't know Mrs. Cohen," Dominique said, "and you have so much going on at home, with the wedding and all, why did you go to her party?"

Jones sank back down on the brocade sofa. "I, uh . . ."

Davis resumed his seat as well. "Why, ma'am?" he pressed.

Jones didn't answer. Davis began to fidget, and finally looked over at Dominique again. He nodded in Jones's direction.

"I can imagine you had a million things to do," Dominique said softly. "I just wondered, if you didn't know the lady, why you gave her so much of your precious time?"

"She . . ." Jones's eyes began to look like Bambi's, caught in the headlights of a car. "Wilfred insisted."

"Why?"

"I had originally said I would go, but then I changed my mind. I wanted to call her and apologize, but Wilfred said that wouldn't be Christian. He said it wouldn't take long, since it was only a half-hour away, and we would only stay for a while." Her voice had taken on a higher pitch, and she coughed softly. "Oh," she said, putting her hand to her throat. "I am so parched. Would anyone like a drink?" She stood up again, and looked at her watch. "No, I'm sorry. I can't offer you that drink. I'm late for a fitting. I'm going to have to ask you to please leave now."

At a signal from Davis, the four detectives put on their coats. "We may need to ask some more questions," Davis said. "And we'll call your boyfriend."

"Please don't bother him," Jones said. "I've told you everything. This incident is just so terrifying."

Jones's eyes, in Elliot's opinion, said that she was more terrified of what the good reverend might think.

"We'll make it brief, ma'am," Davis said, smiling. Shariah Jones didn't smile back.

* * *

Davis glared at the door angrily. "Didn't she say she'd be here?" he asked Elliot. "Are you sure you got it straight?"

"Yes. Three o'clock." He looked up the street. "I think she's coming now."

The two men watched as Erin Feldman parked her minivan in the driveway. Three children tumbled out, running for the back door, giggling all the way.

Davis grumbled but didn't interrupt while Mrs. Feldman disappeared around the back to usher the children inside. She came through the house a moment later and opened the front door.

Her large eyes were full of apologies. "I got stuck in the carpool line," she explained. "I didn't mean to keep you waiting. Please come in."

Davis's impatience barely waited until they were all seated. "We're here to ask you questions about Mrs. Cohen's death," he said. "We understand you fought with her and her party."

Mrs. Feldman blinked her eyes, looking almost like a sad puppy. "That's true."

Elliot spoke more compassionately, to stave off what looked like incipient tears. "Can you tell us what you argued about?"

"She didn't want me to be president of Sisterhood. I was angry."

"Angry enough to kill her?" Davis asked.

"No, of course not. I would never hurt anyone."

Elliot gritted his teeth. The man's interrogation strategy ranged from purely professional to short-tempered snarling. The temptation was almost overpowering to throw him a bone to gnaw on so he'd leave Mrs. Feldman alone.

"Could she really have blocked your election?" Elliot asked.

"She threatened to resign from Sisterhood if I was

elected. Some of the women were afraid she'd do it and take all her friends with her."

"Who?" Elliot asked. He'd had no luck finding out who Mrs. Cohen's friends were. He'd hoped to question some of them, even if they weren't at the party, to find out if they knew of anyone who had ever threatened her.

Mrs. Feldman blinked. "I'm not really sure."

"What did you hope to accomplish by arguing with Mrs. Cohen?"

"I hoped to convince her that I am really Jewish. She is the only one I know of who doesn't accept my conversion."

"Did she agree with you?"

"No. She said that a screaming shrew like me obviously wouldn't make a good president even if I were really Jewish." Her face was bright red. "She made me so mad!"

"What did you do about it?" Elliot asked.

"Do? I didn't do anything. What could I do? It was the same when I was little. Kids used to call me names because I was chubby. What could I do about it then? It wasn't like logic or humanity came into it." She looked helplessly at the two detectives. "So I left. And my husband wouldn't come with me, which made me angrier. I took the car and left him there."

'Did you come right home?"

"What does that matter?"

"It was found that Mrs. Cohen was most likely poisoned after three-thirty," Elliot said. "You left at two-thirty. We need to know if you went straight home."

"No."

"Where did you go?"

"Are you asking me if I went back and went to the kitchen door and gave her poison? No, but I can't tell you where I went, exactly. I was at the mall."

"Did you buy anything?"

"No, I didn't."

"Did you see anyone you knew?"

"I don't know." She looked frustrated. "I didn't know I'd need an alibi. There isn't anything else I can tell you."

"If you think of anything else," Elliot said, noting that Davis's eyebrows were raised, "call us."

"I will."

Davis seemed pleased when they walked down the porch steps. "I think we may have something here," he said. "Maybe we can wrap this up by the end of the week."

Elliot wasn't convinced. "We'll see."

Chapter Thirteen

"Elliot, do you have a minute?" Wally asked. She'd been relieved when he answered the phone, since she'd missed him several times the day before and she really needed to talk to him before she went to work.

"Yes."

"I have to make this quick," she continued. "There is a strange person following me."

"What? Tell me about it." Elliot's voice was all business.

"I saw him for the first time in the coffee shop on Grove Street. He sat behind me when I had lunch with Louise. Then she went back to work, and I went to the grocery store, and he was there, and then I went home, and he was in a car behind me and slowed down when I pulled into the driveway."

"Maybe it was coincidence, and he was just letting you get in before he drove by."

"I don't think so, although I did at the time. I had to go to the post office yesterday morning before school, and he was there again, although I'm sure he wasn't parked on the street or anything before that. Then I saw him outside the butcher shop after school. I'm not a nervous sort of person or anything, and I was ready to chalk it all up to kismet, but then he tried to strike up a conversation."

"About what?"

"Brisket. He told me about his grandmother's brisket and how great it was and how no one ever made it that way anymore. Then he started talking about the movie stars who were in town recently."

"What did you do?"

"I pretended I forgot something and went back in and talked to Murray, the butcher, hoping the man would get tired and leave, which he eventually did. Murray only wanted to talk about the murder and all the movie stars who were in town that day. That was when it occurred to me. This guy may have something to do with it."

"Did you manage to get his name?"

"No."

"He could be dangerous," Elliot said. "Stay away from him. If you see him again, call me."

"I tried yesterday, all day."

"Oh, was that you? I was told that some lady kept calling, but wouldn't leave a message."

"I didn't want to tell anyone but you."

"Right. Well, we're only doing local interviews today, so I'll be in town." Elliot's voice got official again. "Call me if you see that man again."

Throughout the morning, Wally found herself reminded of the murder. First, one of her pupils, the little girl who often bragged that she had the "bestest" of everything, didn't show up for school. The classroom was quieter, since there were no squabbles caused by her boasts. Wally imagined the next synagogue-catered event, and how different the preparation would be without Beverly.

A little later, at snack time, one of the children decided that the apple juice was bad. Wally had a sniff of it, but could not be sure, so she poured a few drops into a paper cup and tasted it. At the same time, the child who complained said, "See, it tastes bad, doesn't it?" It had tasted fine to Wally, and she decided that the child was only noticing a brand change, but she got goosebumps thinking about whatever it was that Beverly ate.

Just before the children got ready to leave, one of them

turned to another and said, "My friend's mommy went to heaven. I hope that doesn't happen to my mommy." Wally decided she'd better talk to the nursery school director.

The conversation took a long time, and left Wally feeling as if a coating on the thin veneer of her students' innocence was gone. She pondered it on the way home, trying to figure out a way to restore it. But her mind wandered, and she found herself thinking about the man who had followed her around town. Her mind strayed back to when he sat behind her at the diner while she talked to Louise about the murder.

That was it, she realized, the thing that had been bothering her. She made a snap decision, and drove right past her driveway, heading back to town.

It took several minutes for Wally to find a parking space, since there were not only the production vehicles for the movie in town, but also several vans from various news stations. She had to park three blocks from the center of Grosvenor, and nearly decided to go home. But when she turned the corner onto Grove Street, she saw that the grubby, strange man was sitting in the window seat at the lunch counter of the diner.

Ignoring her promise to Elliot, Wally went in and sat on the stool right next to the man. She ordered coffee and, since she'd had no lunch, a doughnut.

The order arrived without any conversation having started. In fact, their only interaction was a smile passed as Wally sat down. But there was no question in Wally's mind that the man recognized her. So, taking the bull by its proverbial horns, Wally looked him directly in the eye and said, "Who are you and why are you here?"

He feigned puzzlement, unconvincingly, Wally thought, and smiled again. Close up, he was even slimier than she'd expected. "Look," she said. "I have a feeling that you are investigating Beverly's murder for some news organization. I don't think it's for television, because somehow I think I've seen all the reporters on all the different stations. Sorry to say this, but you just don't look the type. So it must be for the newspapers, although there is an outside chance it's for radio." She broke her doughnut in half. "Considering how tongue-tied you seem to be, my money is on the newspapers. Which one?" Popping a piece of doughnut in her mouth, she awaited his reply.

"Your deductive reasoning is interesting," he replied, "but you failed to consider something else. Did you ever think of tabloids?"

Wally fought the urge to make a face, but the man's next comment told her she had been unsuccessful.

"Ah, a wave of revulsion. Are you sorry you started this conversation?"

She swallowed, considering his question. "I'm not sure. Maybe. But what I want to know is, how did you know about it before everyone else? You were here *before* it made the newspapers and TV."

"You are observant, but you still fail to consider the possibilities."

Wally thought for a minute, stirring her coffee unnecessarily. It gave her something to do while she puzzled over the cat and mouse game in which she'd become involved.

"It was you," she said, forcing her mouth closed after it sprang open. "There was no mention in the news that Bev's death was murder until you leaked it to the media."

The man's self-righteous look surprised Wally. "It needed to be revealed."

"The people's right to know?"

"Yes."

"Why?"

He looked frustrated.

Wally couldn't decide if that look was caused by someone who'd wanted to be a bona-fide reporter but found himself selling sleaze, or, if it was because the man knew something but couldn't reveal it. She weighed the probabilities.

Suddenly it seemed very important to get this man to tell her what he knew. "I'm sorry. I've been rude. Let's start over. Although I suspect you already know this, my name is Wally Morris. What's yours?"

"Tad Seymour." He looked at her closely. "You don't look like the type of person to have solved that serial murder case last year."

Wally chose to let that remark pass, although she got shivers when she realized how much this strange man knew about her. "Why would you be interested in this? Bev is, or should I say was, hardly the tabloid type. Is it that she hung around with movie stars? She really didn't, you know, it was more like she thought she did."

Another silence ensued, only interrupted by the sound of their bulky coffee cups clinking against their saucers as they were put down. She was getting nowhere, except full to overflowing with coffee, with an accompanying set of jitters. The doughnut had turned out not to be worth the calories, and the remaining half sat abandoned, getting even staler on her plate.

She had hoped to get some idea about the circumstances of the media leak from Seymour, but so far he was just toying with her.

There was no approach but the direct approach. "Why did you leak the story to the media?" she asked. "Aside from doing what you consider to be a public service, what could you possibly have to gain from it?"

Seymour's eyes glittered. "I'm paving the way for my fortune."

"How?"

"I don't think I'm going to tell you," he said. "I'm finished here. I'll see you around." He threw some money on the counter, picked up his jacket, and left.

She paid for her own order and rushed after him. There were too many unanswered questions. She caught him at the door, shrugging his jacket on before going out into the cold air. "What are you going to do now?" she asked.

He turned toward her, but he stared at something over her head. She followed his gaze, and saw the cast of *Stalking Sunrise*, staring back at her. Movie cameras were all around, and she heard someone yell, "Cut! Who let these people walk in here?" Four people rushed toward her and escorted her away from the front of the restaurant. She looked for Seymour, but he had disappeared, leaving her alone in her embarrassment.

One of the people who held her arm apologized. "It isn't really your fault. The director just saw a shot he wanted and decided to try to get it. I knew we should have cleared the area."

The explanation didn't make Wally feel any better. She hurried to her car and drove home.

Elliot kept silent all the way up to Darwich, Connecticut. Davis seemed particularly edgy, fidgeting in the front passenger seat. His endless chain-smoking filled the car with fumes. Marlboro. A manly smoke, held between yellow-stained fingers with the most bitten nails that Elliot had ever seen.

"Are we almost there?" Davis asked his partner. Brady was tagging along and driving because Dominique had to testify in court, and they'd had to cancel the interviews that were set up for their team. "It seems like we should have gotten up to the exit by now."

"Only a little farther," Brady said. "Exit Fifteen. The Merritt Parkway. Then just a few more exits."

"A swank town," Davis said. "Several notches up from your little Grosvenor. I'll bet they pay their policemen more."

Alone in the back seat, Elliot repressed a smile, thinking about what Dominique would have said if she had heard that politically incorrect word.

Elliot had promised to tell Dominique everything about the home of Melanie Jensen and Tim Hawthorne. He had also promised to fill Debbie in. It surprised him that both women were so fascinated by Jensen. Sure she was beautiful, talented, and wealthy, with a successful, gorgeous—Dominique's word, not his—husband. Sure she had adorable twins, a boy and a girl, who had been on the covers of every woman's magazine almost since they were born. Sure she had a lifestyle of the rich and famous. What was the big deal?

"This is our turnoff," Brady said. He steered the car along the exit ramp and onto the connecting parkway. The road became more scenic, and, since the trees were all bare this time of year, Elliot got occasional glimpses of the backs of some large homes. Davis snorted. "Some people got nothing to do with their money but put it into their houses."

His voice held such deep disgust that Elliot briefly wondered, as they exited the road and wound through the streets of Darwich, exactly what Davis thought was a good place to put his money. He knew very little about the man, just that he had a reputation for sticking with an investigation until he had it figured out. And for doing it his own way.

"We're here." Davis was practically out of the car before Brady had it in park. Elliot let Brady get halfway out of the car, pulling his bulk behind him, before jumping out himself. Then he walked up the long front path behind both men, taking in the wintry landscape on what appeared to be a large piece of wooded property.

They were greeted at the door by a uniformed maid. She led them into a huge, warm, fire-lit room with blond-paneled walls. Several large plaid couches and club chairs dominated the room and were almost totally covered by stuffed animals. It appeared that the furniture had been arranged around children's indoor play equipment. The raised fireplace, while covered by a protective glass door, was also gated from little people.

In the middle of all of that, almost indistinguishable from the stuffed animals, were two small children, about two-and-a-half-years-old, and a strikingly beautiful chestnut-haired woman. She embodied the image of the perfect suburban mother—her well-scrubbed face shone and her hair was in a ponytail. Her clothes looked like offerings from the highest-priced mail order catalogue. In the most forthright manner, she stood up as the officers were led into the room, and offered her hand.

"I'm sorry my husband is not here right now," Jensen said. "He had to make a run into the city. I would have called to tell you to reschedule, but he told me to go ahead. He said he'd come out to your office if you need him too."

Jensen was tall and well-toned. Her bones, features, and skin were so perfect that she looked like a porcelain figurine. "I hope you don't mind if the children stay with me. I'm away from them so much that the time we have together is extremely important to me."

Davis frowned. "I wouldn't want to say anything in front of them that could be frightening. It would be better if they waited outside."

A pout crossed the actress's lips. Elliot was impressed at how devoted she was as a mother, but he agreed with Davis. Otherwise, they'd have to spell everything out, like Debbie's sister, Rachel, and her husband, Adam, did around little Jody.

"We'll be as brief as we can, Ms. Jensen," Elliot said.

Jensen squatted down beside her children and talked to them quietly. They clung to her momentarily, giving her hugs, before she motioned for the maid to take the children out of the room. She called after them, promising of fun later, before turning back to the men.

With a sweep of her hand, she invited the officers to sit on the couch opposite her. Her starched white blouse, which was open at the throat and accented her lovely skin tones, set her off from the busy fabric of the sofa and the surrounding stuffed bears and rabbits. She bent her chino-clad knees and grasped her ankles, looking at the detectives with interest.

The three men sat uncomfortably among a bunch of stuffed marine mammals and birds. Davis perched on the edge of the couch next to a killer whale, and Elliot sat with a walrus pushed into his back, while Brady squashed a pair of puffins almost to extinction with his ample rump. Brady asked preliminary questions as Davis chafed, waiting for his turn.

After the questions about her name and occupation, Jensen sighed. "I'm really not sure how I can help you," she said in a melodious, honey-filled voice. There was no accent, the kind of American English that gives no betrayal of the place of birth of the speaker. At the same time it was cultured, leading any listener to believe that this was a woman of good breeding. "I really didn't know Mrs. Cohen."

"How did you come to be at her party?" Davis asked.

"I'm not sure. She had invited several people from the film we're about to shoot. I guess that's why I was included."

"But you say you didn't know her."

"That's true. I knew her husband slightly. He examined me for the film's insurance."

"You were not friendly with him either?"

"No."

Elliot chastised himself for acting like a star-struck fan and got down to business. "Why did you go to the party?"

Jensen blinked her emerald-green eyes. "My agent suggested that we attend, since the others were going. He felt that it would go a long way toward increasing goodwill in that town, since we're shooting there, as well as increase interest in the movie. We thought it would only take a little time away from our family so I agreed. That seems now to have been a mistake."

Davis wrote something on his pad. "Did you see Mrs. Cohen at the party?"

"She greeted us at the door. I saw her later, as well. But she didn't circulate much."

"Did you eat at the party?"

"Oh, certainly. The food was very good."

"Did you see Mrs. Cohen eat anything at the party?"

Jensen frowned and nodded. "I heard she died of poisoning. It's so sad."

Elliot would have liked to ask another question. He

wanted to know if she had seen anyone else give food to Beverly, but the detectives had decided to avoid asking that question at this stage. They felt that if someone volunteered that information, it would have a lot more credence. Unfortunately, no one had.

"Yes it is," Davis said, although his voice lacked any emotion at all. "That's why we are asking about whether people saw her eating."

Jensen put her finger to her lip pensively. "I don't know how she would have eaten anything unless it was while she was putting it on the trays. When I saw her from the kitchen door, that's all she was doing. You'd think she would have had that little woman who was helping her do the trays, so she could at least see people while she served them."

From everything Elliot had heard of Beverly Cohen, that was the last thing she'd want at a party she threw. As Mrs. Morris had explained it, Beverly was the hostess, not the hired help, and she'd rather be hidden in the kitchen than have people think she was a server.

"I don't know how she put up with that waitress," Jensen added. "She practically rolled her eyes when Beverly told her which tray to take out next."

"Do you mean Nancy Goldstein?" Davis asked.

Melanie shook her head. "I don't know her name, but she seemed not to like Beverly at all." She furrowed her brows, then turned to Davis, wide-eyed. "You don't suppose she hated her enough to kill her, do you?"

"We'll find out," Davis said. He closed his notebook. "I think we've taken enough of your time. Have your husband call us so that we can just tie up a few loose ends."

Chapter Fourteen

Wally was already on the third aisle in the grocery store, just rounding the corner to go up the fourth aisle, when she spotted Janet Finkelman entering the store pushing a shopping cart. The attorney wore jeans and tennis shoes with an expensive ankle-length trench coat and a small handbag that no mother of small children would consider adequate. It was strange seeing the woman there on a weekday morning because Wally was sure she had heard that Janet had a job with a New York law firm. Knowing it would be appropriate to ask about Bev's family, since Bev and Janet were so close, Wally looked for an opportunity. She had just about worked out her opening inquiry when she nearly ran into Janet's cart in front of the juices.

"Hello, Janet," Wally said, flashing a smile up at the black-haired woman. It wasn't that Janet was so tall, Wally knew, but that she herself was so short. "I'm Wally Morris. I, uh, knew Beverly."

"Yes, I remember," Janet said. "You were at the funeral and you came to pay a shiva call. How are you?"

Janet hadn't moved from Doug's side while Wally and her friends paid a condolence call during the family's seven-day mourning period called shiva. It impressed her that Janet remembered her visit. "I'm fine, thank you. But

108

I was wondering about you. I know that you were very close to Bev and her family."

A grimace passed across Janet's face. "I was. And I am. I'm helping out, during this time. That's why I'm here. I have to shop before I pick up the younger one at ballet. She didn't want to go but I told her that it's paid for and she shouldn't waste the money."

Wally wondered if Janet had given any thought to how difficult it must be for the child, having lost her mother. Apparently the money was of more concern.

Janet glanced at the clock over the produce section and began to push past Wally's cart. "I have to hurry. I don't want to be late. If I am she'll go back inside and I'll have to get out of the car to get her."

She had pushed off before Wally could say anything else, which was probably good, since she was afraid it would sound like criticism. When they passed each other in subsequent aisles they only smiled the way people do when they keep meeting in a grocery store. One simply could not have a whole conversation each time, but Wally felt unfulfilled by hers. There were a few questions she would have liked to ask about the investigation into Bev's murder, but she hadn't been able to. With any luck she could ask Elliot soon. He and Debbie were coming to dinner on Friday night.

It frustrated her that there wasn't much she could do to help on the case. She didn't have access to any of the police information or the people involved. Although it was depressing, she realized that she would just have to sit back and let other people work on finding out who killed Beverly. It wasn't so bad. She had plenty of other things to do. Next week she had to sit for Rachel's little Jody while her parents went on their first vacation since the baby was born. Wally and Nate looked forward to giving the new parents time to enjoy their Caribbean cruise. Relaxation was so hard with a toddler in the house.

At home, Wally thought about all the things she would do with Jody when she visited. She let Sammy out for a run while she unpacked the groceries, thinking it was too bad that it was so cold out, because it would have been nice to take the baby to the zoo. But she was sure she'd find other activities for Jody, as long as they met with Rachel's and Adam's approval.

Sometimes they acted as if they invented parenting and Wally's years of experience counted for nothing. It was so different from the trust that Nancy and George Goldstein had in Wally, but she understood. Rachel had always been very demanding.

The Labrador scratched at the door to be let back in. He generally liked cold weather, but there was a layer of ice on part of the backyard and he would just as soon keep his feet warm. Wally gave him a biscuit which he played with for a few minutes, throwing it up and down before settling down to chomp on it. He acted just like a big baby, and Wally was still laughing when she answered the ringing phone.

"What's so funny?" Louise's voice demanded.

"Nothing. The dog. How are you?"

"Well, I'm fine, but some people aren't."

"What?"

"Nancy has been arrested."

Wally felt the bottom drop out of her stomach. "For what?"

"For Beverly's murder."

"That's absurd."

"I agree! It seems to me that the police were getting pressure to make an arrest, and since no one else popped out as a strong suspect, and it's been over two weeks, and since Nancy was helping with the food at the party, and since she and Beverly had fought publicly last year, they decided to arrest her." A gasp for air signaled Wally that Louise was finished with her explanation. Too bad it didn't really explain anything.

"I thought they made up."

"I guess they sort of did," Louise said uncertainly, "but maybe there was still some friction between them."

The whole discussion was making Wally angry. "You're not telling me that you believe this, are you? What about all the other people who had friction with Bev? What about her friend Janet?"

"What about Janet?"

"What if I told you that I saw her shopping in the grocery store for the Cohens and that she was helping to take care of the family?"

"Where's the housekeeper?"

"How should I know? That's not the point."

"What is the point?"

Wally was losing her patience. "Weren't you the one who told me that there was talk of an affair between her and Doug?"

There was silence on the other end, during which Wally picked up a dishcloth that had fallen to the floor before Sammy could wrestle it into submission. "Are you still there?"

"Yes," Louise said. "I'm just thinking."

"Well, do it louder."

"Okay. I was thinking that it didn't seem likely that Janet would kill Beverly."

"It isn't any less likely than Nancy doing it, is it?"

"But Janet and Beverly were best friends!"

Wally stamped her foot, which scared the dog. She bent down to apologize with a pat on his head, and spoke more softly. "Think about what you're saying. If they were really best friends, would Janet sleep with Doug? Would any woman sleep with her best friend's husband, if they were really friends?"

"I guess not."

"Listen," Wally said, already forming a plan of attack. "I'm going to call Elliot and find out why they think Nancy did this. There has to be a mistake."

"Good. Let me know what you find out. Meanwhile, I'll see what I can find out on the grapevine."

* * *

For the fifteenth time in a half-hour, Elliot answered his phone, expecting either another reporter asking for details of the arrest, or another irate citizen complaining about Nancy's impending indictment.

It was the latter, but at least it was a familiar voice. "How are you, Mrs. Morris? I'm looking forward to dinner on Friday."

Dinner and all Mrs. Morris's fabulous food seemed to be in jeopardy, however, as soon as she explained the reason for her call.

"How could you arrest Nancy Goldstein?" she asked. "She couldn't have done it! What about all your other suspects?"

"We've interviewed them all and there don't seem to be any loose ends as far as they are concerned. The one person who was seen arguing with Mrs. Cohen, Erin Feldman, was cleared by an ATM at the Short Hills Mall. The next customer made a positive ID on her." When they got that information, Elliot recalled, Davis immediately decided they had eliminated everyone but Nancy Goldstein. Now Mrs. Morris was questioning the arrest.

"Mrs. Goldstein's fingerprints were on the garbage bag where the poisoned canapés were found," Elliot explained.

"Of course they would be. She's the one who had to clean up after the party. That doesn't prove anything."

"Also," he continued, "she is the only one who had access to food at the party, and also the only one who would know how to get the poison."

"What do you mean?"

Elliot explained about the Japanese cooking course. He didn't tell Mrs. Morris that when they obtained a search warrant they found a set of knives that Mrs. Goldstein claimed she had been required to purchase for that course. Traces of the toxin were found in the wooden handle on the one she identified as a fugu knife. There was no way to determine how long they had been there.

"That's ridiculous," Wally said. "Did you question everyone about the poison?"

"Actually, no. What would be the point? Should we say, 'By the way, do you know how to extract the poison from a pufferfish?' "

"I would hope that detectives know how to get information better than that. Did you find someone who sold the pufferfish to Nancy?"

"No. We've asked every single vendor who carries it. Imports are strictly regulated by the U.S. Food and Drug Administration, so we know who sells it. No one has done business with any of our suspects."

"Maybe someone bought it for one of them."

"It's possible. We're still checking."

"Did you find the container the poison was carried in among Nancy's things?"

"No."

"So you're saying that you arrested Nancy because you don't have any other suspects?"

"That is not what I am saying. There is ample evidence that she committed the crime. We had probable cause. We'll have all the rest of the evidence by the time of the trial." Elliot paused, giving himself a moment to calm down. "The arrest was not totally unreasonable. Did you know that Nancy lost a catering contract for that office park because of Beverly, two days before the party?"

"What?"

"Nancy had no other source of income, and it was Bev's business that picked up the contract."

"How did that happen?"

"There was an allegation of unsanitary food conditions."

"And, if I may ask, where did that allegation come from?"

Wally's tone had turned decidedly sarcastic. Elliot had to try very hard not to antagonize her. "We aren't sure, but it looks like Bev may have had something to do with it and Nancy knew about it."

"So that's the motive?"

"Don't you think it's reasonable? The woman lost her livelihood."

"But she had her husband's income," Wally argued.

Elliot sighed. "He's been out of work since December one."

There was a gasp on the other end of the line. "I can't believe it! Are you sure?"

"Yes, Mrs. Morris."

"She never said anything." Wally was quiet for a minute and when she spoke again, her voice had lost its strident tone and she sounded more like herself. "Now that you mention it, though, I did notice that George looked pale at the rabbi's party when we were talking about her job being a second income. I can't believe she wouldn't tell me that."

"Some people don't like to mention their misfortune to acquaintances."

"We are far more than mere acquaintances," Wally said. "Are you sure that Nancy knew what Beverly did?"

"We are sure she knew she'd lost the business and why, and we have a statement from the company she was working for that they told her Beverly was the one who got the new contract. We aren't certain she blamed Beverly for it."

"Then you don't have a motive! If she didn't know, she wouldn't be trying to seek revenge."

"We don't actually need a motive," Elliot told her. "But think about it. Nancy might have figured out that it was Beverly. After all, she was right there to pick up the pieces of the lunch business."

"Even if she knew that Bev picked up the contract, which you aren't sure about, there aren't that many caterers around," Wally said dryly. "It might have seemed only logical that she'd get the contract."

"Maybe . . ."

"Elliot Levine, how could you, a soon-to-be law school graduate, think there will be enough to even hold Nancy?"

Elliot resisted the urge to ask Mrs. Morris where she got her law degree.

"Are you still there?"

"Yes, ma'am."

"Why did you decide that the other suspects were not responsible?"

"I really can't divulge that information."

"I understand that you can't tell me anything, but I was just wondering, since Nancy is a friend and all and I'd like to help her, why you decided that none of the other people, who Beverly herself said shared their food with her, were the ones who gave her the poison?"

"Could you be more specific?"

"Okay. As you recall, Beverly said that everyone, with the exception of Louise Fisch, Barbara Fine, and me, had given her something to eat. Right?"

"Yes," Elliot said, wondering where she was headed. "And we used that information to question all the other people at the party."

"Well, what I want to know is, what did they say?"

"We asked everyone, including the actors, who all said the same thing. Apparently it is not uncommon for people to try to snatch things from famous people to have for themselves, and Beverly may have embellished that to make it sound like people were feeding her."

"All of them?" Wally asked.

"More or less."

Wally didn't say anything, but Elliot knew the conversation was not over. "You seem to want it to be one of the show business people," he observed.

"They don't live here in our town."

"You are showing a bit of bias," he said, as lightly as he could.

"It's just that. . . ."

"Look, Mrs. Morris, I understand how you feel. But I really have a lot of work to do." As gently as he could, he tried to get her off the phone, listening as patiently as possible while she listed other suspects and possible motives.

"You have to leave this to me, Mrs. Morris," he said. "I hope you understand it's my duty."

He could hear sorrow in her voice when she spoke. "Can I go see her?"

"She has to talk to her attorney and prepare a case."

"But she can have a visitor, can't she?"

"Family members."

"I'm practically family."

"I don't know."

"Can you find out?"

Nancy's ashen face seemed to have shrunk overnight. Her eyes were wide and scared, as she glanced around the small jail visiting room. Her lips trembled as she walked into the room where Wally sat at a wooden table, and she wore a simple county jail-issued smock.

"I can't believe this is happening," she said, as she slid onto the wooden chair opposite Wally. "How could this be?"

"It's a mistake," Wally reassured her. "The police will find that out and you'll be exonerated. I'm so sorry. If there's anything I can do to help, you must tell me."

"George is . . . We don't have the money for bail. My attorney said I could go home if we did, but we don't."

"I'll get it," Wally said. She had informed Nate that they would post bail if necessary, as she ran to this meeting that Elliot had arranged. Nate didn't argue. In fact, he'd been the one to arrange for the attorney.

Nancy wiped her eyes and blew her nose. "We can't thank you—"

"Forget about that. Tell me anything you can think of so we can clear this up."

"My attorney said not to say anything."

"I understand. But I'm trying to help you, not get you into bigger trouble." Wally fought to control her frustration. "Tell me about other people, what they were doing. It should help us figure out who did it."

"That's just it. I was so busy, I didn't get a chance to notice anyone. I could tell you about all the empty plates I had to clear, and how many times I refilled the platters. But not what people did."

"Elliot told me they found your fingerprints on the same garbage bag where they found some poisoned canapés. I told him that made sense, since you had to clean up, and didn't prove anything."

Nancy wiped her eyes again. "It's so good to know that you believe me."

They talked for a while longer about Nancy's children, whom Wally had visited and brought little presents to cheer them up. But no amount of gifts could replace their mother, and Wally grieved for them.

Too soon, the matron signaled that their time was up. "We'll get you exonerated," Wally said, her own voice trembling. "I promise."

"So you're still here," Wally said. She sat on a stool next to Tad Seymour, who was hunched over a cup in the coffee shop. "I would have thought that now that there's been an arrest, you'd be off to look under different rocks for some new news."

"Hmph."

"What newspaper can I read your version of the story in, or do I have to read it while standing on line at the grocery store?"

"You could buy one of the tabloids. Millions of people do."

Wally wasn't getting anywhere in her conversation. But she had to keep trying, because she suspected that Seymour knew a lot more than he was saying about the murder, and might be able to clear Nancy. "I guess my old friend Nancy is a murderer," she said.

Seymour finally put down his coffee cup. "You can't seriously believe it?"

Ignoring the question in his voice, Wally said, "They must have enough evidence, or they wouldn't have arrested her."

"What makes you think it was anything other than an arrest made to appease the public and the press? They were screaming bumbled investigation."

This time Wally was the uncommunicative one. "Hmph," she said, mimicking Seymour.

"What does that mean?"

"You said 'they' instead of 'we.' " The counter waitress came over and Wally ordered a coffee, sensing Seymour's eyes boring into the side of her face. "You're not a member of the press corps?"

"I don't consider myself one of them."

"You shouldn't put yourself down."

"Very funny. I thought you came to find me for a reason. I must have something you want."

Wally tensed. "Do you?"

"I might."

It was Wally's turn to gape, wishing she could read the little toad's mind. "You have information that would clear Nancy?"

Seymour stared into his coffee cup. "I didn't say that."

"What do you have?"

"I might know something about someone else which would put that person higher on the suspect list."

Wally almost fell off her stool. He had practically admitted that he knew who murdered Bev. "What is it?"

"Do you seriously think I'm just going to give it to you?"

She wanted to scream, but kept her voice steady. "I was hoping you would."

He shook his head. "No way. This is my ticket out of the tabloids. I'm gonna cash in."

With an effort Wally asked, "What about the police?"

Seymour raised his eyebrows. "What about them?"

"What if I told them that you have information about the murder and you aren't giving it? It's a crime to thwart an investigation, you know."

"You can't prove that. Number one, I wasn't there," he ticked off on his fingers, as he made each point. "Two, I wasn't even invited, and three, I have no motive."

There had to be a way to get him to talk. Wally tried to think of one while she waited for another point to be enumerated, but couldn't. A thought occurred to her. "You knew her, didn't you?"

"I met her," Seymour said simply.

"Where?"

"At a benefit."

Wally was surprised, but it opened up some possibilities. If they were connected through the movie star end of things, it meant it wasn't through people who lived in town. And if Seymour really knew something about the murder, didn't that mean that the person who did it was someone other than Nancy? "I wonder why she didn't invite you to her party."

Seymour shrugged. "I guess I'm not the type to throw a big expensive catered party and require her services."

"Is that really why she invited those movie stars?"

Seymour smugly sipped his coffee. "Isn't it obvious?"

"But why did they go?" Wally asked. "Wouldn't that be the real question?"

With a sneer, Seymour said, "Supposedly, it was because it would generate goodwill among the uptight people of your fair city. But," he narrowed his eyes, "it was probably because of their secrets."

Wally stopped playing with her spoon and put it down. "Who had secrets?"

Seymour raised his eyebrows again and looked at her, reminding her almost exactly of Stacey, a little girl in her class who said, "I know something you don't know," on a regular basis. That was rarely true, but Wally suspected that Seymour wasn't just bragging.

"I imagine," he said, "based on the rumors that I've heard, that all movie stars have secrets." He waved his hand. "In fact, every one on the cast of the new movie has secrets, and I know all of them. I've made it my business to be sure about this. But the one whose secret I knew only because of Beverly will have to remain anonymous."

"So you admit it?" Wally said.

"What?"

"That you caused the murder. It happened because of

something Beverly told you. You were probably trying to get verification of some sort and the person found out."

Seymour furrowed his brow. "I guess if you put it that way . . . ."

"But how would the person have known that Bev told you whatever it was, or even that you knew her?"

A wry smile crossed Seymour's face. "People would have seen us talking. I know for sure that a lot of people saw us together because at the end of our conversation we made kind of a scene."

"You've got to tell the police! It could be the whole basis for the case! You know who did it and why."

The vindictive Seymour came back. "Possibly. But I won't go to the police."

Wally looked at him. "If you aren't going to tell me what this is all about, why are you even talking to me?"

"Because you are in the middle of this and people around here seem to believe what you say. If I am to get any recognition at all, and regain my credibility, I need you to know that I had the information first."

"Okay," Wally said, feeling as if she were talking to a kindergartner, "I'll tell people you knew it. You can come forward and clear Nancy."

"No."

Frustrated, Wally asked, "What are you going to do now?"

"Research." He waved an airline ticket folder in front of her face. "I'm going to write a bestseller. With any luck, and the continued incompetence of the local police, it'll be ready by the time the arrest of the right person is made. I'm hoping for a really big sale."

Chapter Fifteen

Wally savored her second cup of morning coffee slowly, to make it last, while pondering her dilemma.

Tad Seymour had hinted that Beverly knew something about one of the people on *Stalking Sunrise*, and that might have made someone angry. If it was really something big it might even make that person angry enough to kill. Seymour had also said that they each had a secret. But how did Beverly get involved with that?

It had to be through Doug.

Wally was interrupted in her musing by the ringing phone. Elliot's voice sounded different, less adversarial, as he asked how she and Nate were.

"We're both fine," Wally said, after thanking him for returning her call of the previous evening. "I realize you're in a hurry with all the important things you have to do. I just wanted to talk to you about the case you have against Nancy."

"Okay."

"I know I've already told you this, but I'm sure she didn't do it. I've been going over the list of suspects, and I have a few questions."

"Shoot."

Wally took a deep breath. "Bev knew something that was supposed to be secret about one of the movie stars."

"What secret could she possibly know?"

"Don't you know what her husband does for a living?"

"Yes," Elliot said. "He's a doctor, why do you ask?"

"Because he examines those movie stars."

"I know that. That was how Beverly met them and came to invite them to the party."

"Right. But on occasion she had been known to tell little secrets to people about various movie stars that her husband examined."

"She did? But he shouldn't have told her anything about the people he examined."

"Of course he shouldn't have. But either he did or she read his files. And she used to brag about it. She'd say things like 'I can't say who it is, but guess who had her nose done,' or 'Guess whose pouty lips came from her thighs?' "

Elliot was quiet for a minute. When he spoke again, he seemed to have given consideration to her theory. "So you think she told this Tad person something very private about someone who came to the party and that will lead us to the killer?"

"It's just a theory," Wally said, wondering if she sounded too melodramatic. "But maybe you could interview them. Supposedly they each have some secret."

"Really?"

"That's what Tad says, I think. He was being pretty cryptic, but I'm sure that's what he meant. You should ask Doug Cohen."

"He has already told us he cannot discuss his patients."

"Oh," Wally said. "Then can you go see those people?

Elliot was quiet again.

Wally pressed her point. "We need to be able to ask these people questions, or poor Nancy might end up in jail forever, or worse."

"Hang on a minute. I'm not disagreeing, I was just thinking about a strategy. You're right. We didn't ask all the right questions. I'm going to do it."

"Great!" Wally said. "Let me know what you find out."

She felt more hopeful than she had in days. She planned to tackle Doug herself, as soon as she figured out what to say.

"I wish I could have gone on every single interview," Dominique said when they left for the first re-interview. "I feel like I only have about half of the picture."

"I feel the same way," Elliot said as he steered the car.

"Okay, so where are we headed?"

"To Brooklyn." Elliot selected a lane. "We are going to see Kevin Cole." He changed lanes and avoided the merge for traffic going to the Garden State Parkway, heading instead down past Newark Airport. As usual for this time of day, the Pulaski skyway was jammed and the roads leading to the Holland Tunnel had backed up for miles onto the exit ramps. Elliot and Dominique had plenty of time to talk while they inched forward between stop lights to the tollbooths.

"The reverend was an interesting character," Dominique said, speaking of Shariah Jones's new husband. The wedding, which was less than two weeks after the murder of Beverly Cohen and had more than two thousand people in attendance, had been covered extensively by the media, with a special spread exclusively in *People* magazine. "He is the most self-righteous man I've seen in a long time. Everything is strictly black and white with him, and right or wrong. There are no gray areas, or areas that might get a little mixed. It's a wonder he even lets Shariah act in movies that aren't PG."

Elliot shrugged.

"I guess he doesn't want to give up that money she brings in," Dominique added. "He told us that she tithes twenty-five percent of her gross to his church."

"Wow. That must be a bundle. What does he do with all that money?"

"He uses a lot of it for his broadcast."

"What broadcast?"

Dominique laughed. "I thought you knew everything.

Every Saturday afternoon the reverend interviews people on Newark cable. Usually it is to promote one of his pet causes, which a lot of times is abstinence. He'll get someone on who believes there is room in the world for responsible imbibing, then he jumps in with one of his sermons, and the other person might just as well have stayed home, for all he gets to make his point."

Elliot saw an opening in the traffic and zipped into it. "That doesn't sound like fun."

"I think you're right." Dominique scowled and it wasn't at the traffic. "I was thinking, do you know how old Shariah is?"

"I believe she is twenty-four, why?"

"That's what I thought too. Which is why what the reverend said was so hard to believe."

"What did he say?"

"Well, he was acting like I was the only one in the room, and talking only to me. The county guy was kind of ticked, but he understood that the reverend was unwilling to talk to him. Brady kind of set me up to ask questions and nod my head a lot when he went into one of his little sermons."

"So?"

"So one of his mini-sermons was about his favorite topic, about how people should never touch a drop of the devil's brew."

"Come again?"

"Alcohol."

Elliot drummed his fingers waiting for Dominique to get to the point. He hated trying to figure out what she was talking about on his own, because he was usually wrong, but she stretched out her stories forever. He inched the car forward when he could, trying to get to the EZ PASS lane. "What is your point about the reverend?"

"He implied that Shariah's lips had never touched wine— or anything stronger. He kept commenting on her purity of spirit."

"I don't believe it," Elliot said. "I heard where she grew up and when she left to go to the west coast."

"Exactly," Dominique said. "I don't believe she never touched a drop of alcohol in her whole life."

"But what does this have to do with anything?"

"It could be a secret that a tabloid reporter was trying to get published."

"But wouldn't there need to be proof?" Elliot asked. "Who would have that kind of thing?"

"What if there was a record of her, I don't know, getting arrested or something?"

Elliot shrugged. "It's possible. But it wouldn't explain anything related to our case."

"True. But maybe there was something else, and maybe when she was examined for the movie, Doug Cohen found out and maybe he told his wife and that was what she was leaking to that Tad Seymour guy."

Elliot nodded appreciatively. "You are one smart lady. That's all possible. Would that make Shariah our killer?"

"I guess it would. I would think she'd do anything to avoid Reverend Purity and Light knowing about her, or worse, the media, especially since the murder occurred before the wedding."

"We'll look into it."

Dominique shook her head. "It would have to be something a doctor would find out during an exam for Bev to be a threat, if Mrs. Morris is right. I wish Doug Cohen had told us something other than his patients' records are confidential. You'd think, since his wife was murdered, he'd be willing to bend the rules."

Elliot, future lawyer that he was, shook his head. "He can't."

Dominique pointed to a shorter line and Elliot pulled into it. After several more delays, they managed to get into and through the Holland Tunnel.

"I wonder," Dominique said, "why Mrs. Morris was designated by that slimy guy as recipient of his information."

"People like to tell her things," Elliot said. "I'm not sure why, although he apparently knew about her detective work last year. Maybe he figured she had a connection to the police. Let's just hope we can figure out a way to use it."

There was a long but comfortable silence between the partners as they inched their way through the dense traffic in lower Manhattan, past City Hall. Eventually they made it over the bridge and down to Brooklyn Heights. The beautiful brownstone-lined streets were just changing over from being full of shoppers to residents scurrying home, and they were able to find a parking spot right outside Kevin Cole's house. He answered their knock immediately and flashed a huge, white, toothy smile.

His eyes fastened on Dominique immediately. "Welcome to my home, Detective Scott," he said, his voice projecting like a stage actor's. Almost as an afterthought, he added, "And Detective Levine."

He gestured grandly toward the interior of the brownstone, and Elliot was reminded of all the wannabe actors who served tables in New York. This was one who had 'made it,' and yet he was still so overblown. Surely his grandness was too much for movies? Elliot concluded that the act must have been for them alone and maybe a few of the passersby behind them on the sidewalk.

"Please come in," he said. They walked down a hallway and turned, past pocket doors that extended all the way up to the twelve-foot ceilings, into a living room. It was dimly lit and sparsely furnished, totally unlike the lavish interior decoration at Heath Maxwell's. The sense Elliot got was that of practiced youth. There were brand new inline skates, and an unused snowboard against one wall. Several magazines geared for twenty-somethings lay on the coffee table, but the corners of a *GQ* and an *Esquire* peeked out from the pile. The stack of CDs next to the stereo had incongruities as well, which made Elliot wonder what was wrong with the picture. He couldn't figure it out, but let the idea go. There was information he needed to get.

"Can you tell us how you knew Dr. and Mrs. Cohen?" Dominique asked. She and Elliot had decided to let Dominique's beauty work for them with this young actor. They had read that he had just had a thirtieth birthday bash, and since they were just a few years younger, they thought they'd go for simpatico. And physical attraction. Elliot watched as Dominique recrossed her long legs languidly, thinking that if her dentist husband, James, saw her in that mini-skirt and knew that he'd suggested that she wear it, he'd probably extract every tooth in Elliot's head. Without Novocaine.

"I already told your partner in our first interview," Cole said, briefly glancing at Elliot. "I barely knew her husband."

"So why did you go to the party?"

"All the stars were going as a gesture of goodwill to the local people, since the movie is being filmed there."

"Was that the first time you met Mrs. Cohen?" Dominique asked.

"Yes. I'd never formally met her before. But I knew what she looked like, since I had seen her at a gathering in New York."

"Did you see who she was with at the event? Other than her husband."

"Yes. She was with one of the sleaziest tabloid reporters in the country."

Adrenalin rushed through Elliot's blood. It was as if they had proof of what Mrs. Morris said. People had seen Bev with the reporter. He couldn't resist the temptation to ask, "Do you have something to hide?"

He was rewarded with another one of those huge smiles. He sensed that it was supposed to be charming, as if Cole whispered "charming" to himself as he flashed his grin. Elliot began to wonder what James would make of all those perfect teeth.

Cole ran his hand through his sun-bleached—or was it peroxided?—hair, and gave his head a youthful toss. Elliot again had the sensation that things were not as they seemed.

"Of course I don't have anything to hide. My life is an open book. But anything a person said could be misconstrued, and then it might end up in the tabloids."

"Even something said at a little party?"

"Said to the wrong person . . . ."

"Are you saying that Mrs. Cohen might have told something to the tabloids? Why would you think that?"

"After I saw her talking to the reporter there were all those rumors."

Dominique looked up from her notebook. "Rumors? Can you be more specific?"

"Yes. There was a rumor about someone on the cast of *Stalking Sunrise*, something that was very sensitive in nature."

"Do you know who it was about?"

"No. I just know that it was some secret that none of the papers would buy without confirmation. I'm sure that Mrs. Cohen was the one who leaked it to Tad Seymour."

"How do you know that?" Dominique asked. Elliot could tell she was holding her breath. He realized he was too. Hearing Seymour's name from a completely different source boosted the likelihood of his story being accurate.

"He's the reporter I saw talking to her. He's also the one who had the story."

"I never heard anything in the news about the cast members. Do you know why the story never came out?"

"Because Tad didn't get the backup he needed for the papers to print it. They don't like losing lawsuits, so they are being more careful now."

"Where do you think he would have gotten that backup?"

Kevin looked surprised. "Haven't you figured this out yet? From Beverly Cohen. That's why she was killed."

"I thought you said you didn't know her? How come you're so sure of the reason she was killed?"

"Who else would kill a caterer?"

Dominique was silent, and Elliot clenched his fists to keep from saying anything. Cole seemed to have forgotten his presence, and sat on his chair ogling Dominique's legs outright.

"If what you're saying is true," Dominique said after a while, "who do you think did it?"

Cole tore his eyes from Dominique's legs and looked into her eyes. "I didn't allow you here to rat on my co-workers," he said, as if he had a choice. "I need something from you."

"What?"

"The way I see it, the only way that Beverly Cohen could get any dirt on the members of the cast of *Stalking Sunrise* was by reading her husband's files. I want to make sure that those won't be brought out in court, at least not for the people who aren't suspects."

"So you do have something to hide?"

"I'm not saying that."

"What are you saying?"

"I just want your word that nothing about me will be revealed."

Dominique scowled. "The doctor's files have a secret of yours?"

Cole's broad smile was back, but his eyes had a tension that contradicted his grin. "Not exactly a secret. It's nothing important. Do I have your promise?"

Elliot spoke up. "Since you so obviously have something to hide, aren't you afraid that we'll consider you to be the prime suspect?"

"Look," Cole said, for once looking sincere. He removed his tinted glasses and rubbed his eyes. "I'm not really hiding anything."

"You're older than you claim to be, aren't you?" Elliot asked, noting that both Cole and Dominique had their mouths open. "How much?"

"Okay," the actor said, "ten years. I'm forty. But at least that secret is not something that could ruin my life or my career, like the secret that Tad is trying to sell."

"The secret is that big?" Dominique asked. "What is it?"

Cole shook his head. "I really don't know. I wouldn't think it could have anything to do with either Melanie Jensen or Shariah Jones. Heath Maxwell's career has been on shaky ground for a long time. I think the only thing that saved it was those cologne ads he does. That's probably how he got the part in the movie in the first place."

"So you think Maxwell is our killer?"

"I don't know. I've given you all I've got. Will you keep my secret?"

"Only if your story checks out."

"It will," Cole said. "Honestly."

Elliot nodded. "We'll do our best."

Cole had given them a lot more to go on than they had. They zipped out of there to look for more.

Chapter Sixteen

"**C**an I serve you some more chicken?" Wally asked, concerned because Elliot had not eaten as much dinner as usual. He'd only had one leg and thigh of chicken, a paltry number of roast potato pieces, three stalks of broccoli, and two slices of her freshly-baked-from-scratch challah. She'd seen him eat more than that when he'd refused one of her dinner invitations because he was on his way to dinner with Debbie.

"No, thank you, Mrs. Morris," Elliot said. "I'm full."

"Challah?"

"No, thanks."

Wally took a quick look at Nate, who seemed puzzled too. When he'd cut off the end of the challah earlier to "taste it," in his weekly excuse to get an early piece of bread, Nate had pronounced it excellent. Now the braided loaf just sat there, still fragrant and delicious, and untouched.

Nate took another piece of the bread with a reassuring look at Wally, who smiled gratefully. The whole meal had taken less than fifteen minutes to eat, and Wally had hoped to linger a little longer and maybe get some information at the same time. She assumed that Elliot had gone to investigate Seymour's lead, but he hadn't called her, and so far, he hadn't mentioned it. She couldn't just bring it up, that would seem inappropriate, so she kept quiet. "I'll go start the water for tea," she said.

"I'll help, Mom," Debbie said. She and Wally cleared the table on their way into the kitchen.

"What's the matter with Elliot?" Wally asked, while she ran the water into the tea kettle.

"What do you mean?"

"He's acting kind of strange—quiet, and not too self-confident."

"I think he's feeling a little embarrassed," Debbie admitted.

"Why?"

"Because you figured out something that all the detectives couldn't."

Wally shook her head. "I didn't figure anything out. I just knew that since Nancy couldn't possibly have done it, someone else killed Bev. Personally, my money was on that woman, Janet."

"Why?"

"Doug's mistress, or so everyone says. She's not very nice, at all."

"Elliot said that when he looked into your lead from that tabloid guy, he had some confirmation that he may be involved."

Wally could barely suppress her pride. "Is there anything I can say to make him feel better?"

"Just leave it," Debbie said. "He'll bounce back."

The kettle whistled, and Wally poured the water into the teapot. Debbie finished arranging the chocolate chiffon cake slices on the plate and put it on the tray along with the tea cups. She carried it in while Wally brought in the teapot, and together they poured and served.

"This cake is delicious, Mrs. Morris," Elliot said. He sipped his tea and let out a long sigh. He seemed more relaxed suddenly, and, at a nod from Debbie, Wally seized the moment.

"Did you find out anything from my lead?"

"I have to admit," Elliot said, "that I was skeptical about

Seymour's allegation that everyone had secrets. But we've been checking it out."

"And?"

"It may be true. We got something to go on."

Wally almost spilled her tea. "You found something important, didn't you? Can you tell us?"

Elliot was quiet. Wally let him decide on his own, since there were probably rules about discussing the investigation with people outside the police department. But underneath the table, she crossed her fingers.

"Well," he said, "I can tell you that we went to see Kevin Cole."

"What did he say?"

"It wasn't a long interview, but the essence of it was that the gossip item that Tad Seymour was trying to peddle was enough to somehow ruin someone's life. And it wasn't about Cole."

Wally mulled that over while Debbie rushed ahead, trying to pump a suddenly silent Elliot into telling her what secret Kevin Cole had.

"So the murderer had a horrible secret?" Wally concluded.

"I'm not sure that we can jump to that conclusion," Elliot said. "This theory is based on rumor."

Nate put down his tea cup and looked at Elliot. "What is your gut feeling?"

"I think that Cole was telling the truth, and that Heath Maxwell is looking stronger as a suspect."

"Oh, that is so sexist," Debbie said. "Why not one of the women?"

"Well, now that you mention it, my partner, Dominique, seems to think that it's unlikely that Shariah Jones was really the teetotaler that her husband required."

"Based on what evidence?" Nate asked.

"Based on her having been around a bit. Dominique seems to think that Shariah had a past that she didn't share with her reverend. She wasn't religious before, and it seems unlikely she never touched a drop of alcohol."

"What about Melanie Jensen?" Wally asked.

"We've talked to her and she, of all people, seems to have absolutely nothing to hide."

"What's next?" Nate asked. "Will the other detectives join in?"

"The county guys think we're wasting time, since they're sure the killer is Nancy. They want us to forget about these leads."

Elliot cleared his throat. "Dominique and I are going to talk to Heath Maxwell tomorrow, anyway."

"How are you going to ask him if he has secrets?" Wally asked.

"Very carefully."

"This must be so upsetting for you," Wally said in a gentle voice, firmly but solicitously holding Doug Cohen's elbow. "I've heard the rumors."

They stood outside the sanctuary following Saturday morning services. It had nearly broken Wally's heart, watching Doug and his two small children stand to say kaddish for Beverly. Now many people were standing around, avoiding direct eye contact with Doug, and Wally knew that his feeling that he was in a fishbowl would prevent him from shaking her off and walking away. She hated to do it, but she couldn't see any other way of approaching him. A phone call to his house the night before had been aborted due to a number change, and she hadn't wanted to call his office.

Wally gave the unruly left side of her hair a tug to turn it under, and went to talk to Doug.

The young father turned to Wally, and she could see the pain in his downcast eyes. This wasn't the murderer, she thought to herself. If she had any doubts, they were gone. So, it was difficult for her to justify intruding on him during the kiddush, while people all around him were eating mini-bagels, creamed herring, gefilte fish, and cookies, but she felt she had no choice.

There must have been, behind the pain, the slightest

touch of guilt. She realized that Doug might think the rumor she was talking about was his relationship with Janet. She hurried to explain. "I spoke to someone who said that Beverly may have leaked sensitive information to the press. That must make matters even worse."

Doug turned miserable eyes to Wally.

"It's possible, isn't it," she continued, "that Beverly talked to a reporter from the tabloids about a member of the cast of *Stalking Sunrise*? I hear that they all knew about it, but no one was sure who she talked about."

"I heard about it."

It was news to Wally that Doug knew about Bev's slip of the tongue. "When did you find out?"

"A patient of mine told me when he paid a sympathy call."

"Someone from *Stalking Sunrise*?"

"No, another movie. But I don't believe it. It could ruin my career if she . . ." He shook his head. "I can't believe I could still get angry at her." He swallowed. "Why would she do that?"

Wally didn't answer that it was because she'd loved to brag. She waited nervously until he wound down, but before he could move away, she asked, "How would she get that information? Surely you didn't tell her about your patients?"

"Of course not," Doug said. He lowered his head like the little boys in Wally's class who had misbehaved. "Sometimes she waited for me in my office. She did the night of the AIDS benefit, because I was late getting back." His guilty look intensified.

Wally could only wonder if that was because he was with Janet. "But what—"

"She might have seen a file."

"Whose?"

Doug's silent grimace answered the question. "I can't say with any certainty."

"But it could be important," Wally prodded.

"How could it matter now?"

"What if one of the people in the movie, someone who was also at your house the day of the party, was the one she had leaked information about? Then just possibly that person might have been the one who gave her the poison."

Doug's eyebrows were up. "Do you think . . .?"

"As a matter of fact I do. Think about the suspects. Forget Nancy, her arrest was a mistake. I only wish the police could prove that and get her out."

Doug looked grim. "Her children must be as confused as mine."

"I'm sure they are. But, getting back to the people at the party, the other possible suspects, think about them. You've known most of them for years. Can you imagine that any one of them would want to kill your wife?"

"Not unless someone wanted her out of the way," Doug said unhappily. Wally followed his gaze as he looked around to see where Janet was. His face was pale. "You don't think . . . ."

Willing herself to sound unconcerned, Wally said, "If the police don't find out who really did it, I'd think Janet might be the next logical suspect."

The look of alarm on Doug's face told Wally she'd hit her mark. "But I really think it had something to do with your patients," Wally said, giving him a straw to grasp. "What if one of them wanted to stop her from confirming a story before it could be published?"

He shook his head as if to clear it. "I suppose it's possible. But how would I figure out who?"

"Are you saying that more than one of them has a big secret? One that you know about from your examinations?"

Doug jumped. "Why do you say that?"

"That was what I understood the rumor to be."

"Hm. I still don't know how I'd narrow it down."

Wally knew her mouth was hanging open at the news that there were several people with something big to hide, and she hurried to close it. "You're saying that of the four movie stars who came to your house, and were in the cast of that movie, three of them had a secret?"

"Three?"

"We've ruled out one." She whispered into his ear, "Kevin Cole." His face registered a brief smile, as if he was thinking about Cole's secret and found it amusing. Wally wished she could know what it was, but didn't have time just then to speculate. "Are there any more that could be eliminated?"

"I can't say."

"You could, if you had nothing on some of them."

"But if I did, you'd know who I had what you call 'something' on."

"I see. So you're saying you have information on at least some of the others."

"No. I'm actually not saying anything of the kind. How could I? That is all privileged information. If I don't uphold doctor-patient confidentiality, I can kiss my career good-bye."

"But this is your wife's murder we're talking about."

"I'm not trying to protect the killer," Doug said painfully, "and I wish I could help you. I just don't want to leak anything myself." He thought for a moment. "Let me ask you a question. Let's say, hypothetically speaking, two had secrets. How would I figure out which one she talked about?"

Wally wondered who else Doug might have eliminated. "I've been thinking about that. Could she have gotten into your files?"

"No. They are locked away. But if there was one on my desk—"

He broke off, looking more miserable than ever.

"If you knew whose file was on your desk the day that she made the contact with the reporter, maybe that would help."

Doug didn't look convinced, but Wally persisted. "Maybe you could figure out whose file you might have had on your desk at that time, or in the previous days, whenever Beverly was in your office. That shouldn't be so hard to narrow down."

"So you're convinced that the killer is one of them?"

"Uh, not to hedge my bets, but ninety-five percent sure."

"Listen, I'll see if I can find anything out, without violating any confidences. But then who would I tell to get it investigated?"

"Leave it to me," Wally said. She was glad that Dr. Wimp had finally agreed to do something about his wife's murder. "I have a contact at the police department. He is very discreet as well."

"I feel like I should be thanking you. You've given me back some hope of this ending someday. I didn't think that Nancy did it either, and I was upset that she was arrested. But what could I do? And I didn't like thinking that it might have been . . . ."

Wally followed his gaze to Janet. "Don't worry that you might have caused it with your relationship with her." She didn't add, *Not that I condone it.*

He signaled to Janet and started to walk toward her. Turning back to Wally, he said, "I'll call you, soon."

As Wally watched him walk away, she sincerely hoped that he would follow up on their conversation.

Chapter Seventeen

Wally was up well before the sun on the day that she and Nate were going to start babysitting for little Jody. The baby's parents would be off on their cruise to the Caribbean in just a few hours, starting with a flight to Miami. Then Wally and Nate would have the toddler all to themselves.

She could barely wait. She'd spent all the time that she wasn't working, or worrying about Beverly Cohen's murder and Nancy's arrest, getting ready for this week. The nursery school was closed to correspond with the winter vacation in the public schools, so it all worked out. It was too bad that Jody was still such a fussy eater and couldn't appreciate Wally's fine cuisine, but she'd have to make do. She still knew how to boil macaroni and melt cheese on it, like she did when Rachel was small.

Wally made Nate a nice breakfast, figuring it might be just a smidgen harder once Jody arrived. She had no illusions about taking care of a toddler.

Nate poured heated maple syrup over another pancake, and before he put a forkful into his mouth, he said, "I'm glad you have something to take your mind off Nancy's troubles." Wally knew he had more reasons than that for wanting the baby over. He couldn't wait to have Jody all to himself.

They made it to Rachel's and Adam's in less than thirty-five minutes, and found them ready and waiting.

"Momma and Daddy go on a boat," Jody said, dazzling her grandparents with her brilliance.

Wally stooped down to pick up the eighteen-month-old. "Grandma and grandpa can't wait for you to visit," she said, smoothing Jody's red hair. "We are going to have so much fun."

"I don't want you to think that we don't love Jody," Adam said, shaking his own red head on his way out with a suitcase, "but we really need to get away." He took the suitcases and baby things and filled the trunk of the car. By the time everyone was in it, it was positively cramped.

"Too bad you got rid of your van, Mom," Rachel said. "You would have had plenty of space left if you still had it."

"I'm glad it's gone," Wally said. "This car is big enough for me. I'm not like you new mothers with expanding families."

Rachel giggled. "Then why does your car have a car seat?"

"Your father insisted." She smiled at Nate, who had the best seat in the car, aside from Jody's, at that particular moment. He was driving, and so was the only one who wasn't wedged in between carry-on luggage and diaper bags.

"Just remember," Rachel said, "I wrote down a list of instructions, and also a list of her doctor's office, home, and emergency beeper numbers. We prepared a notice giving you the right to sign for treatment, and our wi—" she sniffled, "our wills are in the filing cabinet in the bedroom closet."

Wally took the lecture from her daughter in stride, even though it annoyed her how little faith Rachel had in her ability. It was so different from the way Nancy treated Wally, showing total confidence in Wally's abilities. Several times in the past few days Wally had taken the children to the library, a favorite activity, and to friends' birthday parties. Although she was out on bail, Nancy wouldn't leave the house, and her husband had interviews for possible jobs that he just couldn't afford to miss. The children looked lost, as if their worlds had shattered, which was almost true. Nothing was the same. Their mother, though she was still physically present, had changed. She was barely recognizable to them. Hopefully, since Wally was going to be so busy, friends would pitch in and include Nancy's children with their own plans. Wally had dropped several hints in what she hoped were the right places.

She set aside that sad subject to focus on her family. Rachel was doing what any new mother would do, and she did it well. Wally only hoped that her daughter would be able to relax enough on her vacation to enjoy it.

Adam rushed the good-byes at the airport and Rachel was disappointed that Jody didn't wake up to let them say good-bye to her. She slept peacefully through the scurrying to unload the car and the hunt for tickets. The car was quiet all the way out of the airport.

Then the baby awoke and screamed for her parents the rest of the ride home.

Debbie called soon after the baby went down for her afternoon nap. "How's it going, grams?" she asked. "Want some company?"

"Sure. Will Elliot be coming too?"

"I don't think so. You've got him kind of tied up. He said he was going to check out your theories."

Wally had to add guilt that Debbie was missing Elliot to the mountain of worry about Nancy. She could only hope that this would be over soon. "Let us know what train you'll be on and Dad can pick you up."

Sunday afternoon, Dominique invited Elliot in to have a cup of coffee with her husband while she changed out of her church clothes. James had already changed into jeans and a Howard University tennis team sweatshirt. He shook Elliot's hand less than enthusiastically and led him into the den where a pre-game show was just starting.

"You're going to miss the hockey game," James said. "It's supposed to be a good one."

"I'm sorry that we can't watch it. The last one was great."

"Too bad you can't stay." James's voice was cold, so different from his usual warm and friendly tone.

Elliot was nervous. "Dominique explained, didn't she? We have to check this out, both for the sake of justice, and for our careers."

"I understand. I just wish someone other than my wife could take care of it."

Sweat trickled down Elliot's back. "She says she wants to do this."

"I do," Dominique said from the door to the hall. She had changed into a suit, and pulled her long hair into a French braid. "James, we've been over this." She picked up her jacket, shoulder pack, and gloves and led the way to the door. "See you later, hon," she said. But it wasn't her usual "hon."

Elliot was quiet, too afraid to talk while Dominique was angry, which was most of the way to the Lincoln Tunnel. Finally, as they wound their way down toward the toll booths, Dominique broke the silence. "Does Debbie object to this as much as James does?"

"No. Her mother is the one who started it, so I guess she wouldn't."

"It's not just that James is worried about me," Dominique said. "I think he's also lonely. I haven't been spending too much time with him lately."

"This will be over soon."

"So you're convinced that Heath Maxwell is the killer?"

Elliot headed over to the east side. "It doesn't matter what I think—we have to prove it."

They arrived at Maxwell's building and asked the doorman to ring his apartment. "Is he expecting you?" the uniformed man asked.

"Not really." He flashed his badge. "But I think he'll agree it's important."

The doorman examined the badges carefully before he pressed a button on his panel and spoke into the telephone. "He said you can come up. Do you know the way?"

"I do," Elliot said. "Let's go."

Maxwell, larger than life as usual, opened the door when they rang the bell.

"May we come in?" Elliot asked.

Maxwell seemed to be looking for Inspector Davis. "I interrupted my Sunday afternoon for a couple of kid cops?"

Dominique bristled. "We're detectives on the Grosvenor police force."

"Hah. A town that can't even pronounce its own name right. Well, we can't stand here with the door open letting everyone hear my business. Come in." He waved them into the living room of his apartment. Maxwell indicated that they should sit on the couch. He chose a seat opposite them, hiking up his pants legs before he sat, revealing argyle socks, which Elliot was willing to bet cost no less than $75.

Dominique did not sit right away. She walked over to the sideboard where there was a display of Viceroy, the cologne that Maxwell was a spokesman for. It had the appearance of a shrine, in Elliot's opinion, since most of the bottles and boxes seemed to be encased in plastic.

"I've never smelled this cologne," Dominique said. "I hear it's extremely strong." With that she opened the one bottle that was not part of a sealed set.

"Don't do that," Maxwell shouted. "Quick, close it up."

Instead of running to do it himself, Maxwell ran into the bedroom. Dominique did as he said, and turned to Elliot, looking about as puzzled as he felt. The scent had just reached where he was, a strong one, not to his taste, when they heard Maxwell ask if it was closed yet.

"Yes," Dominique said.

"Open a window."

"I guess he doesn't like it either," Elliot said, as he lifted the shades of two windows so he could open them. A cold wind blew in and soon the scent of Viceroy was gone.

Maxwell finally returned to the living room. "You shouldn't have done that," he said. He seemed to be wheezing a bit, and perspiring as well.

"I'm sorry," Dominique told him.

Elliot thought that no matter what, Maxwell's reaction was out of the ordinary. When he took a look at the actor's face, to look for some clue about it, he thought for a moment that there was something wrong with his eyes. Maxwell's face was swollen and he had angry red welts running from his chin downward, disappearing under the collar of his sweater. At Elliot's raised eyebrow he sighed. "Don't worry, I used the epi-pen. I'll be all right in a few minutes."

"Let's sit down," Elliot said. When they were seated, he asked, "Can you tell us what just happened here?"

"I can tell you it has nothing to do with that poor woman—what was her name, Beverly Cohen? I thought the police had made an arrest."

Dominique shook her head. "We're not convinced that the lady who was arrested is guilty."

"Well, innocent until proven guilty, I say," Maxwell said.

Dominique seemed to disregard the statement. "There is doubt that she had sufficient motive. In fact, the motive is considered to be an attempt to suppress information that had been leaked to the tabloids. Nancy Goldstein, the accused, has nothing to do with anything like that."

Maxwell slumped in his chair.

"Did something ring a bell?" Dominique asked.

"Like what?"

"Like the rumor," Elliot said. "We've been informed that everyone in the cast of *Stalking Sunrise* knew there was a nasty rumor going around that could affect someone's career."

"Don't get snide with me, Robocop," Maxwell said. "I had nothing to do with the murder."

"But you have something to hide," Elliot said.

Maxwell nodded. "I think you can see for yourself what that is."

Anyone could see, Elliot thought. "You're allergic to the

product you hawk. And that product is one of the major backers of the film, your comeback movie. Dr. Cohen knew about this, but I'm willing to believe he was one of very few."

"He prescribed the epi-pen for emergencies such as the one your partner caused," Maxwell admitted.

"I'm sorry," Dominique said again. "But I understand. If that came out, your career could be over."

"That's right. Is it going to come out?"

"Only if it pertains to the case," Elliot said. "Does it?"

Maxwell sighed. "Look, let me be honest with you. I knew there was a rumor. But it wasn't about me."

"How can you be so sure?"

"I know because I . . . I swore I wouldn't discuss this with anyone."

"You could discuss it in open court if you prefer," Elliot said.

Maxwell looked at Dominique with a pitiful plea in his eyes. She leaned forward and said, softly, "We'll keep it quiet if we can, but we need to know how you know it wasn't about you, so we can eliminate you as a suspect."

Impossible, Elliot thought, but he took Dominique's warning glance to heart, and remained quiet.

"I know," Maxwell said, sighing, "because I paid Tad Seymour ten thousand dollars to find out. He assured me that the story wasn't about me."

"And you believed him?"

"Well, yes. I have him over a barrel, so to speak. He can't publish anything about me now, or I'll produce a cancelled check. The only way I'd pay him was by check, for that reason, so I could show that he accepted money regarding a story." He turned to Elliot. "I'm not as stupid as you seem to think I am."

"Can you prove that?"

"I have the cancelled check in the vault, but I have a photocopy of it right here." He strode to the desk and took out a piece of paper. It showed both sides of a check, endorsed by Tad Seymour and cancelled by his bank, five days before the murder.

"Did he tell you who the rumor is about?" Dominique asked after she examined the check.

"No, sorry."

Elliot was deflated. It made sense, yet it shot his theory. He had hoped to wrap up the case today yet they were no closer to finding the killer than before.

Dominique flipped a page in her notebook. "If you wouldn't mind, we have a few more questions."

"Okay."

"Do you know, independently of Mr. Seymour, who the secret is about and what it might be?"

"No to both questions. And I don't want to know. Whatever it is, I'm sure it isn't the public's business."

"That's it then," Dominique said.

As much as he hated to concede the point, Elliot had to admit that Dominique was right. He glanced over at the Viceroy shrine one more time, as if it were the villain. But there was no such simple answer—not here, anyway.

Chapter Eighteen

"She's so adorable," Louise said, holding little Jody on her hip. "Doesn't she go with my hair? She could be mine."

"Perish the thought," Wally said.

Louise giggled. "I don't mean my daughter, I mean my granddaughter."

"Wouldn't you like to be an in-law first?"

"Yes, of course. But it's been a long time since mine were little. I'm ready for the next stage."

"Too bad your children aren't."

"True. But just look at how nicely she fits. Of course, that probably means that I need a diet."

"Don't worry about it," Wally said. "You look fine."

Jody squirmed. "Go down."

Louise put her on the floor reluctantly. "Okay, honey." Without taking her eyes off the little girl, she asked Wally the next question. "How are you coping?"

"The baby has only been here for a half-hour."

"I not a baby."

"You're right," Wally said. "You're a big girl."

"I don't mean with Jody," Louise said. "I know you've been snooping around trying to find someone other than Nancy to take the rap for Beverly's m-u-r-d-e-r."

Wally smiled at Louise's spelling a word in front of

Jody. She hadn't forgotten that part of childrearing. "Did you say take the rap?"

"You know what I mean."

"Well, yes. And I have been doing a little, uh, research."

"What did you find out?"

Wally watched as Jody tried to throw a ball. "Do you remember me telling you about a man who was following me?"

"Yes."

"I talked to him."

Louise tore her eyes from Jody long enough to stare at Wally open-mouthed. "What?"

Wally explained what she learned from Tad Seymour. "Now Elliot is investigating."

"Alone?"

Jody rolled the ball toward Wally who missed it because she had turned to face Louise. "No. Dominique Scott, his partner, is doing it with him. But the county people are convinced they have their killer, and they won't lift a finger to help, even with background checks."

"Background checks?"

"If there are secrets that caused this whole thing, a little bit of history could go a long way toward revealing them. Since Elliot and Dominique are in this alone, everything is taking longer."

"So did Elliot find anything out?"

"Not so far, and he's seen almost everyone."

"Is he seeing Melanie Jensen?" Louise asked.

"No. He ruled her out. He's positive that she couldn't be the one who killed Beverly."

"Yes, she could," Louise said. "She was in the kitchen."

Wally watched Jody go over to a table where an early picture of Rachel and Adam was displayed. The baby smiled and clapped her hands. "Look at Mommy and Daddy!"

"That's right," Wally said. She turned to Louise, to make sure her friend saw what a bright granddaughter she had.

But Louise was scowling, as if waiting for Wally to respond to her statement.

"I know Melanie was in the kitchen," Wally said, "but Elliot is sure she couldn't have done it."

Louise cocked her head to one side. "Don't you remember that Tim Hawthorne mentioned that they weren't going to come but that Melanie suddenly decided she wanted to attend. Doesn't that sound suspicious?"

"Yes." Wally turned to Louise and sighed. "Her husband did say that. I'll tell him again."

"I am right," Louise said, apparently pleased with herself.

A while later, Nate brought Debbie in from the train. After greeting Wally's daughter and asking a few pointed questions about Elliot, Louise excused herself.

She and Wally went out to the curb where her two-seater was parked. "I hope Elliot finds something. Keep me posted."

Wally turned back toward the house and saw Debbie holding Jody in the window, making the baby wave bye-bye. Maybe Elliot would come over and talk to them about his latest investigation results. She decided to call and invite him. At the same time she'd remind him about Tim Hawthorne's remark, and mention that Louise remembered it too. Somehow that made it more significant.

"Now where?" Dominique asked, when she and Elliot were back in the car. "So far we aren't having any luck."

Elliot snapped his seat belt, wishing he'd been the one to drive. "Maybe the rumor wasn't what caused the murder."

"What made you jump to that conclusion?"

"We've eliminated the male actors who were at the party, right?"

"Agreed."

"Then if the rumor reason is true, that only leaves the two female stars. And you don't really think one of them did it, do you?"

"Who said?"

Elliot was quiet. Dominique's tone put him on his guard. Her implication was clear—a woman could kill as easily as a man, if not better.

She seemed to be waiting for an answer. "What do you think?" he said.

"I haven't ruled out those women."

Elliot studied his partner. "So you think that Shariah Jones poisoned Mrs. Cohen?"

"I didn't say that."

"That would leave Melanie Jensen. But that doesn't make sense."

Dominique turned her large brown eyes toward Elliot, momentarily taking them off the road. "Why not?"

"The woman has everything in the world she could possibly want."

Dominique's right eyebrow rose. "Tell me again about what was said during the interview with her."

Elliot related the events as clearly as he could remember, but Dominique didn't comment when he was done. In fact, she was silent all the way back to New Jersey.

James greeted them at the door. "Wally Morris called looking for Elliot."

Dominique and James went into the den while Elliot went into the kitchen to return the call.

"Hi," Wally said. "I'm glad you called back. I wanted to remind you about something I mentioned to you, and stress its importance. When I told it to you it was just a recollection, but my friend Louise reminded me about how odd it was at the time. She said that Melanie Jensen's husband specifically stated that they weren't going to come but suddenly his wife decided they had to attend. That might mean she found out about the rumor and came to stop Beverly from telling people about it."

"Um, hm." He didn't sound convinced.

"Is that all you have to say? Aren't you going to check it out?"

"We're checking everything. You'll have to trust me."

There was a long pause. Then Wally asked, "Could I please talk to Dominique? I want to apologize for disturbing her husband."

Elliot called out for Dominique. He held his hand over the phone while he explained what Mrs. Morris wanted. She nodded and he handed her the receiver.

"Hello," Dominique said warmly. Then she listened for a while. "Really?"

She turned puzzled eyes toward Elliot. "I understand. You may be right. I'll look into it."

"Good-bye." Dominique hung up and sighed.

"What did she say?" Elliot asked.

"Oh, nothing really."

"It sounded serious."

"It was just about, um, recipes."

"Recipes?"

"Yes, she said something about since I was out all day it might be nice to make something special for James tonight. I think she's right. I don't mean to run you off, but I'd like to get started."

Elliot said good-bye, not without noticing that he hadn't been invited to dinner. Worse, even though it kind of sounded like Mrs. Morris was about to invite him when he first talked to her, she hadn't either. And worst, he knew Debbie was there.

"Where are we on this case?" Captain Jaeger asked, when Elliot and Dominique arrived in his office the next morning.

Dominique looked at Elliot before turning back to Jaeger. "We're following a lead."

"What?"

"A real motive."

"Nancy Goldstein had a real motive. Revenge. It's as old as the Bible."

"I think the one we are working on may have been stronger," Dominique said. "The murderer may have been trying to prevent Mrs. Cohen from confirming a secret about herself that was likely to end up in the tabloids and cause real problems."

Elliot, forming the opinion that they were on a wild goose chase going after the movie actors since they'd turned up nothing, kept silent, waiting for Jaeger's response.

He shook his head. "Herself? You think it was a woman?"

The two detectives responded simultaneously.

"Yes."

"No."

"Oh," Jaeger said, "so you disagree with each other. Then why should we waste time on this? So that we can look like idiots? We have a suspect already."

"Captain," Dominique said, "we have eliminated some of the possibilities and we would like to interview the other two."

"Who did you talk to?"

Elliot filled Jaeger in on the encounter with Kevin Cole. Dominique told him about Heath Maxwell.

"Sounds thin," Jaeger said. "What am I talking about? We have a suspect and the investigation is closed."

"But it can't be!" Dominique said.

"Are we letting our emotions take over?" Jaeger asked her sarcastically.

"Captain," Elliot said, "you're not being fair."

"Look," Dominique said, "all I'm trying to say is that we can't let an innocent woman go to jail for something she didn't do, while a guilty person goes free."

Although he wasn't convinced they were on the right track, Elliot agreed with Mrs. Morris that Nancy Goldstein was not the killer. They would probably have to start the investigation all over again, but what else could they do? "Sir," Elliot said to Jaeger, "that wouldn't be fair or ethical."

"Elliot, you're young, an idealist, and a law student. You won't get very far in this world by bucking the system."

Unable to control himself, Elliot said something he'd

promised he'd never mention. "Is that so? Just exactly how did you get to be promoted?"

Jaeger pounded his desk. "This isn't the same."

Elliot's frustration exploded. "No? It isn't like when you used your own vacation time, and money, to fly to Florida after that con man took that old lady's life savings? It isn't like the time you infiltrated the protection racket that was being conducted in town? Then what's it like?"

"Calm down." Jaeger, who had jumped up, sat back down. He took a minute to look at the two detectives. "Okay, maybe it is."

Jaeger pushed his pen set closer to the center of the desk and straightened the angle of the pens. His eyes made brief contact with each of the detectives in front of him before he stood up abruptly. Pointing to the door, he said, "Go find the killer."

Chapter Nineteen

Dominique drove on the way to see Shariah Jones. When they got to the tree-lined street that was her new home, they planned what they would say.

"I think I should approach her alone," Dominique said. "If my guess is correct, this is highly sensitive and she'd never discuss it with you."

Elliot agreed, cooling his heels outside the house while Dominique spoke to the movie star. After nearly half an hour, Dominique came out. She held her hand at her side on the way down the steps but as Elliot looked up at her, she gave him a thumbs up.

"Tell me," he said, as they threaded their way through Branch Brook Park and headed for the Garden State Parkway.

"She didn't do it."

"How can you be sure?"

"She had already told her secret to the one person to whom it mattered. Wilfred."

"What? Before the murder? Then why did she go to the party?"

"He made her go. He said that since this woman had broken the barriers between them—a lie that could have cost them their marriage—they couldn't disappoint her."

"That's incredible. Then the secret couldn't have been so bad if he forgave her for it."

"Well, it was bad enough, at least in her mind. But he is a good man, and he understood. He said purity of spirit could overcome a stain, and she had enough purity to overcome hers."

"What was it?"

"It isn't essential for you to know."

"Dominique! Give me something convincing!"

She sighed. "No one else hears this."

"I promise."

"Including Mrs. Morris."

Elliot nodded. Dominique was quiet, possibly because she was choosing her words, and Elliot knew that it was better to let her phrase it the way she wanted than to try to rush her. "It wasn't so horrible, really. When she was very young, living in California, she got drunk and ran her car into a tree. That's how she got that little scar above her eyebrow. Dr. Cohen had specifically asked her about it and she had told him the whole story."

"That would look awful in the tabloids," Elliot said. "Can you imagine? Preacher's wife drives drunk as wild teen."

"It wasn't like that," Dominique growled.

"I understand," Elliot said, nodding agreement. "Most tabloid stories are misquoted events. But maybe the reverend was afraid that's what would be printed and he is the one who poisoned Beverly."

"No."

"No? How can you be so sure?"

"Shariah didn't tell him until they were in the car on the way over. He couldn't have gotten the poison."

Elliot felt he needed to understand this. "Why was she going in the first place? She doesn't seem the type to do it just for publicity reasons, like some of the others."

"She planned to try to find a minute alone with Bev to plead with her not to confirm the story, if the story of the rumor was about her."

Dominique sounded convinced, but Elliot continued to press her. "So why did she confess to the reverend?"

"When they were in the car he kept asking her what was wrong, and she realized what their marriage could be like if she didn't tell him. She had him pull off the road, and explained the whole thing. That was why they were a little late."

They continued in silence. Possibilities were being eliminated, and few leads were panning out. While Elliot felt Nancy was innocent, without the real killer she was still facing trial and potential conviction.

Elliot was lost in thought as he drove to Darwich, Connecticut. Dominique asked him what he was thinking.

"Maybe we should be looking more closely at Janet Finkelman," he said. "Mrs. Morris seemed pretty sure she's some kind of witch."

"She also seemed pretty sure that it was one of the actors, based on what Tad Seymour told her."

"That hyena? He's probably saying that to make himself sound important. He can't get famous with his big secret, since someone killed his source before he could get it confirmed. Maybe there wasn't even a secret to begin with."

"Elliot, listen to yourself. We've had confirmation from at least three people that there was a secret. Why are you being so bull-headed?"

He didn't answer.

Dominique turned the corner. "You could be wrong, you know."

"We'll see."

By the time they pulled up in front of the Jensen-Hawthorne home, Elliot had real misgivings. His wish to make the interview quick so he could go back and review evidence against other potential suspects led him to go along with Dominique's request to do most of the talking.

"I'm afraid you'll have to wait," said the uniformed maid who answered the door. "Ms. Jensen is with the wardrobe fitter for the new movie. She will be a few more minutes."

"This place is gorgeous," Dominique said, while they

waited in the same room that Elliot had been in before. She pointed to some pictures on the mantle of Jensen and Hawthorne with their children and some plaques for Jensen's efforts on behalf of several charities. She looked all around, and said, "This is my idea of the perfect home."

"Thank you," said a voice. They both turned and saw that Jensen, wearing a rose silk robe, had come in through a door opposite the one they had used. "I'm so glad you like my taste."

"It's lovely, Ms. Jensen," Dominique said. She introduced herself, and reminded the movie star of her meeting with Elliot. "We are just trying to tie up a few loose ends."

"I heard that you arrested someone."

"Yes," Dominique said, "you are correct. Someone was arrested, but the investigation is continuing."

"I see. So you are questioning everyone again?"

"No. Just the actors."

"Why just us?"

"Because a source has suggested that one of you may have been trying to prevent Mrs. Cohen from revealing a deeply personal secret."

Jensen looked horrified. "Is that so? What a terrible thing. Although, I have to say it seems unlikely. My co-stars are all very nice people."

Dominique pressed on. "We'd like to have an understanding of exactly what you did at the party."

Jensen put her hand to her chest. "Me? I guess I did the usual things one does at a party."

"Maybe we should sit down," Dominique suggested. She sat opposite Jensen, but Elliot remained standing, silently.

"Please just tell us what you were doing that afternoon," Dominique said.

The actress twisted a strand of her chestnut hair, giving the question some thought. "Well, I was mingling with the people that Mrs. Cohen had invited."

"And eating?"

"Some. I guess I ate some of the food. It wasn't really to my taste."

"Oh, what kind of food do you like?"

She stopped twisting her hair and put her hands on her knees. "Just this and that. Basic all-American food, nothing exotic. I prepare simple broiled fish and vegetable dishes because I have to watch my figure. The public expects it."

"So you didn't spend any time alone with Mrs. Cohen?"

"I already answered that when the other police officers were here."

"I'm sorry," Dominique said. "I wasn't able to be here. Could you please tell me what your answer was?"

"No. I did not spend any time alone with her."

Dominique looked puzzled and referred to her notes. "But we have a witness who said that you visited in the kitchen with Mrs. Cohen and that your husband mentioned that you weren't going to attend the party but suddenly decided to go."

"That isn't true. Is your witness a woman?"

"Yes."

"Ah, that explains it. You see women are always so drawn to my husband because he is very good-looking. She probably got distracted and misheard him."

Dominique straightened up. "What is the secret that you are trying to conceal?"

Aghast, Jensen said, "I beg your pardon?"

"One of our sources said that each of the stars who went to the party had a secret," Dominique explained. "We have talked to everyone else, and now we'd like to have an understanding of yours."

Melanie Jensen clenched her hands into tight balls. "How dare you accuse me of hiding something? You are beginning to sound like a reporter for one of those damned tabloid newspapers. Always trying to dig up some dirt, making allegations with no basis." She turned her head away, staring at some distant point. "From the time I was a teenager they've been following me around like stalkers, watching me, asking people about me." Her voice trailed off as her monologue, first seemingly aimed at the police officers, became increasingly inwardly turned.

But suddenly she looked up and smiled. "I don't know why I let it get to me. Maybe I'm feeling a bit like poor Princess Diana." She stood up and, turning away from the detectives, stared out the window for a full minute.

She turned back to face them, with tears filling her eyes. "It must be those nude pictures I posed for as a teenager. I was so young and foolish and—"

She bit her lip. Taking a deep breath, she continued, hesitantly. "I immediately regretted it, but I couldn't get them back." Spent, she sank down into the sofa. "There, now you know the awful truth. Are you satisfied?"

The maid entered the room and signaled that someone was waiting. Jensen's brow unfurrowed and she stood up. "I'm sorry. I know how important this is and I hope I helped you. But now I must run. The maid will see you out." She walked out of the room, with a straight proud back.

Elliot shook his head when they were back in the car.

"That's pretty much what she said last time, although she seems not to have liked the food at the party as much as she told Davis. The nude photos confirm the story of each of the stars having a secret but I don't believe anyone would have killed a person over something like that." He grimaced. "We aren't any closer to the killer. We still don't know who or why. And we're running out of time before the trial."

Since the weather was warmer than usual for early February, Wally took Jody for a walk into town. They looked at all the store windows, and greeted quite a few of Wally's friends.

Even though it was midday the streets were full of people. She assumed they were there because of the movie. Mobile trailers and vans, wire cables and food trucks occupied every square inch of space except the area where the filming took place. On one block Wally and Jody stopped to watch part of the movie being made. Heath Maxwell walked out of the post office ten times, exactly the same way. After a while, most of the crowd that was watching got bored and moved away.

While Wally pushed the stroller past the flower shop Jody fidgeted with her bagel. Wally bent to break it in half, so that if the little girl dropped it there would still be more. When she stood back up, she bumped into Tad Seymour, who was carrying a briefcase with an airline ticket folder sticking out of the side pocket.

He jumped, then he scowled.

Noting that he had overreacted, and lacked his usual smarmy self-confident attitude, Wally took a close look at him. His shoulders seemed to be hunched and his constant glances, around the street and back down at her, reminded Wally of a pigeon.

"Are you going somewhere?" Wally asked, nodding in the direction of the ticket.

"N-no. No, no, no."

Jody seemed to like that. "No, no, no," she said.

Seymour looked at the child as if she were an alien.

"My granddaughter," Wally said, by way of explanation.

"Very nice." Seymour turned away. "I have to go."

"Trying to catch a plane?"

He looked confused. "What? Oh." He glanced at the ticket. "No, I already went. Research, you know."

He scurried off like the white rabbit, leaving Wally wondering if he was deranged. Maybe nothing he said had any meaning at all.

The phone was ringing when Wally and her granddaughter got home. Wally answered it while taking off Jody's jacket with her other hand. She had not forgotten how hard it could be to juggle children and phones. Of course it was a lot easier, now that she had a portable phone.

"Hello, Mrs. Morris?"

The voice that greeted her was very familiar. Wally and her family had become close with Elliot's partner, Dominique, and her husband, James.

Wally gripped the receiver. "Tell me what you've found out so far."

Dominique told her that they had re-interviewed both Jones and Jensen. "I really can't say what Shariah's secret was, just that both Elliot and I believe her. And Melanie's was not so terrible, certainly not worth committing murder over."

"Oh?"

"She said her secret was that she posed for nude pictures as a teenager," Dominique said. "We're checking into whether they've ever been published. That wouldn't be something to kill for."

"I agree," Wally said. But she didn't believe it. Not only was that not something medically-related that Doug Cohen might have known about, Jensen was a twig when she was in her teens, before she disappeared from public view. The Calvin Klein-type androgynous pre-pubescent ads didn't become popular until much later. She told Dominique as much.

Wally had an idea, and she told Dominique about her latest encounter with Seymour. "We have to find out where he went. He may have been doing research on the person he thinks is the murderer. If we see where he went, it may tell us whom he suspects, and give us some clues."

"I'll get back to you as soon as I can," Dominique promised.

Chapter Twenty

"**H**ere's what I have," Dominique said on the phone early the next morning. Wally had just given Jody breakfast and was now cleaning it off the furniture, and out of Jody's ears.

"Hang on," Wally said. She took Jody out of the high-chair and let her walk around in the kitchen, playing roll-the-ball to Sammy. The good-natured black Labrador stopped the ball with his nose and nudged it back toward the little girl. It was a good way to keep both of them busy, while Wally concentrated on Dominique. "What did you find out about Tad's trip?"

"Hold on," Dominique said.

Wally looked over to check on Jody, and gently pulled a dog toy out of her hand before she was able to get it into her mouth. She substituted a board book and sat Jody down to look at it. Sammy lay down next to the little girl.

"I'm back." Dominique's voice took on some enthusiasm. "We had some luck."

"We?"

"Elliot remembers when Melanie Jensen was known as The Sylphid. He thinks you may be onto something. Especially now." Dominique told her where Seymour had visited, and who lived in those places. They ranged from a rural place in the deep south to Hollywood and New York.

162

Breathless, Wally said, "Do you know who he was tracking?"

"Yes."

"Who?"

"Melanie Jensen."

Dominique told Wally her theories seemed to be panning out. "Melanie Jensen lived or worked in each of those places. If there is something to this, it looks like she's our girl."

Wally took a moment to process that. She thought of what she knew about Jensen from news stories, magazines, and gossip she overheard at the salon when she was having her hair trimmed and recolored. She'd have to revisit every bit of it now, based on their suspicions.

"I only wish we had more to go on," Dominique said, sounding frustrated. "But I know that's like wishing we had a smoking gun. It isn't going to happen."

"I'll see what I can find out on my own," Wally said. After she hung up, she put Jody's coat and mittens on. "Let's go to the library," she said, picking up her car keys. "We'll get you some more books."

Five minutes after they got into the library, Wally felt a presence watching her. She held Jody's hand, walked into the stacks, and came upon Tad Seymour.

"Why are you here?" she asked. He looked terrible, twitching nervously, and looking over his shoulder.

"I'm working."

"You could be working anywhere. Why here?"

"I want to be completely up-to-date on every move the murderer makes."

It infuriated Wally that Seymour knew who did it, and why, and wouldn't come forward. "Why are you waiting?"

"I'm betting I can finish my book before the murderer gets arrested. The longer it takes, the closer I am to finishing. No publisher could possibly turn it down." He gestured at a laptop computer in a study space. "I'm nearly there, then I'll let you figure out who it is and maybe the police will actually find the evidence."

"I'm way ahead of you."

His eyebrows raised. "Oh, but even if you're on the right track, which I doubt, you don't have proof, or even a motive."

Wally shifted Jody to her other hip. "I thought we'd established that a personal secret was the motive."

"Yes, but you still don't know what it is. Until you do, you have squat. You don't even know how he or she got Mrs. Cohen to eat the poison."

"Oh, I think that last part is an easy one. Everyone seems to know Beverly's habit of eating food off other people's plates. All the murderer would have had to do was put the poison onto her own food."

Seymour's eyebrows raised. "Her?"

"Yes."

"I'll give you that. But what about the other questions?"

It was Wally's turn to be cryptic. "I'm working on it."

Seymour turned around. "You know where I'll be." He scurried back into his study, leaving Wally on her own.

A while later, Wally had stacks of photocopies, several old magazines, and six children's books for Jody. She was attempting to juggle them all, including the toddler and her diaper bag, when the library suddenly became a very noisy place. She turned to Seymour, who was standing next to her looking through some of the photocopies, to ask him if he knew what was going on.

He shrugged just as the cast of *Stalking Sunrise* entered the library.

Wally dropped her papers and looked over at the counter where the original magazines were all stacked, awaiting return to the archives.

"Let me get that for you, ma'am," Kevin Cole said. His knees cracked as he squatted down and gathered her papers. If he noticed what was on them, he didn't ask.

From her unusual view of the top of someone's head, Wally noticed that Kevin's hair was thinning. She also noticed that his neck was more wrinkled than she would have expected a thirty-year-old neck to look. It made her wonder if she had figured out his secret.

"Thanks," she said. He flashed her a huge grin in response and went back to where his director was putting marks on the floor. Everyone else was asked to leave the library.

When she got home and put Jody down for her nap, Wally called Louise and invited her for coffee. After explaining where she'd been, she pulled out the photocopies and magazines.

The first set were photos of Jensen wearing maternity clothes. "Look at these," Louise said. "I guess they were all done during one photo shoot, because she seems to be the same size in all of them."

Wally looked at the pictures of Jensen in front of her Darwich, Connecticut, home which was fronted by about a thousand tulips. She didn't seem so big, considering that she was carrying twins and it was obviously already late April at least. "When were the babies born?"

Louise scanned down the article. "May fifteenth, almost three years ago."

"Those are early May tulips," Wally said, "especially in Connecticut. It doesn't make sense."

Louise pointed to a paragraph. "It also says they were born in an undisclosed location in Indiana."

"She went to Indiana to have them? That's strange." But it explained why Tad Seymour had included it on his itinerary.

"Maybe she was from Indiana and she went home to have them," Louise offered.

"She was from someplace down south," Wally said, her imagination running wild. "And her husband was from Montana. "So why . . .?"

"Wally," Louise said, "what are you thinking? You have that look."

"Maybe she was faking it."

"How do you fake a pregnancy that produces two kids?"

"Maybe someone else had them."

Eyes wide, Louise asked, "You think they are adopted?"
"Maybe."

"But the boy looks just like his father. I don't understand."

"This is just a theory, so don't look for too many flaws.
Here goes. What if she wasn't really pregnant, but used a
surrogate to have the babies, with artificial insemination of
her husband's sperm? Then she faked the pregnancy so that
she wouldn't have to say that the babies weren't hers."

"Were they her own eggs? Because if they were, the
babies are hers." Louise said as she flipped to another
photo. "I read about a lawsuit like that."

"Let's say they aren't her own. Maybe there's a reason
she can't have her own children."

"What could it be?"

"I don't know," Wally admitted. "But it could be something she didn't want people to know about her. Being in-
fertile is nothing to be ashamed of. It had to be something
else."

"Would it be a big enough secret to poison someone
over?"

"If the theory is right, that she did it, then I would have
to say yes." Wally sighed. "If only we could prove it." She
turned back to the photocopies. There was a lot of studying
to do.

Long after Louise had gone home, Wally studied the
magazines and photographs. While she let her mind wan-
der, trying to formulate a concept of the time surrounding
the events, she turned the pages of the magazines that
showed the pregnant Jensen. Wally saw which other movie
stars were popular back then, who else was dating whom,
and what split-ups were imminent. At the back of the magazine she saw ads for weight-loss supplements, miracle ex-
ercise machines, and lots of other products, some of which
could be purchased far cheaper than at stores.

One item in particular, a Celtic locket, caught her eye.

It was not only pretty, but reminiscent of Jensen's jewelry on the day of the murder. Wally read the ad.

"Envelop yourself with your most wanted scent, anytime, anyplace. Tiny fabric pads concealed in this locket can hold small amounts of your favorite perfume or aromatherapy product. Minute holes that let the bouquet waft through are obscured in the pattern."

Too bad, Wally thought. The locket wasn't watertight. It wouldn't make a good container for poison.

Realizing that she was really reaching, she looked at the web address in the ad, and typed it into her computer. The menu on the site was extensive, but what caught her eye was the listing for poison bracelets and rings.

And what caught her breath, when she clicked on that entry, was the identical bracelet to the one Jensen wore. It had a hinge on one side and promised to have enough room to hold two aspirin.

Or possibly enough poison to kill a woman.

Chapter Twenty-one

"**I** can't wait to hear about your trip," Wally said, after she loaded Rachel's and Adam's suitcases on top of all of Jody's equipment. Her daughter and son-in-law glowed, although Wally suspected that Adam, so fair, may have had a twinge or two from his sunburn.

By the time they drove up to Rachel's house Wally had heard all about the vacation, and Rachel and Adam had been filled in on Jody's antics. She and Nate would miss their little granddaughter.

They carried everything inside and Rachel reached for the thermostat to turn the heat up. "Would you like some tea, Mom?" she asked.

"No, thanks. I want to get going."

"Good," Rachel said. "The pilot told us there is a storm predicted."

Adam looked out the window at the sunny day. "Those weathermen never know what they're talking about."

"Maybe so, but promise me you'll go straight home," Rachel said.

"Eventually," Wally said, longing to leave immediately. She was a little achy after taking care of her granddaughter for a week and Rachel's heat didn't seem to be coming up at all—it was bone-chillingly cold in the house. Reaching into Jody's bag, she pulled out a sweater.

'I don't think she really needs that, Mom," Rachel said.

Deferring to the child's mother, Wally zipped her lips on the subject and got ready to leave. "I'll call you later," she promised.

Once outside, Wally decided that since the sky was bright and sunny and it was unseasonably warm, Adam was probably right. It would be the perfect time to drive to Connecticut, which wasn't all that far, since she was already in Westchester. There was something she wanted to do. She thought about calling home to let Nate know, but he was in the city and his intern/assistant for this year, Cassie, had called in sick with the flu.

Forty minutes later she was in Greenport, Connecticut. She turned onto the main street and noticed how upscale the town was. All the chichi stores were there—Talbots, Benetton, Ann Taylor, Burberry, Williams Sonoma, Coach, and more. It took Wally a few minutes of driving around to find a parking space, but as soon as she did, she hurried to her destination.

The address she wanted was a few streets over, past more fancy stores and a cute little tea shop.

The sky was graying when she found the address. Instead of a regular jewelry store, she found it was more of a museum store. There was a display of books about painters, scarves, ties, and umbrellas in Monet patterns, some stained-glass windows reminiscent of Frank Lloyd Wright and Tiffany, educational toys, and several kinds of jewelry. Wally went to the counter with the Celtic jewelry display.

In one of the trays were some large silver bracelets with garnets set in the middle, exactly what Wally wanted to see. They looked remarkably like the bracelet Melanie Jensen had worn to Bev's party. Wally had to get a closer look, to see if what she was thinking was even possible.

"I'd like to see that one," Wally told the woman at the counter.

"A very lovely bracelet," she said, handing it to her.

Wally reached for the bracelet and put it on her arm. She

would not have picked it for herself, especially since it made her arm look rounder than usual. Yet when Jensen wore it, it looked pretty, especially with her long thin limbs.

There was a more important consideration, though. "How does it open?" Wally asked.

"Like this," the woman said. She snapped open the middle of the bracelet. There was a small bowl within that could have held something the size of a dime. It was possible . . .

Shivers ran down Wally's spine. Had she found the kind of container that carried the poison? If Jensen's bracelet opened like this and she really was the murderer, this could have been where the poison was concealed. How hard would it have been to open the lid, pour the poison onto the food and snap the bracelet shut?

She had to call Elliot or Dominique. They had to find out, if possible, if her suspicions were correct. She wondered how far Darwich, where Jensen lived, was from Greenport. Maybe she had bought it right here.

"Are you interested?" the saleswoman asked.

"I feel like a movie star," Wally said, hoping to trigger some conversation. "But I'm sure a movie star wouldn't wear something like this."

"Oh, but you would be so wrong," the saleswoman said, smiling. "We get several movie stars in here, and I have sold quite a few. Not all exactly this style, but even a few exactly like this one. Young women like them, mostly."

Her implication that Wally might be just a bit too old to wear something like that did not go unnoticed. "It is beautiful," Wally said, forgiving her, because she meant well. "But really, I'm thinking of buying it for my daughter," she explained. "Although I'm really not sure if it's currently in fashion."

"Oh, yes," the woman said. "I sold one just like it to Melanie Jensen, only a few months ago. You've heard of her, haven't you?"

"Yes."

"She bought this exact style."

"I'll take it."

While the woman was wrapping the bracelet as a gift to keep up Wally's pretense that it was for Rachel, she chattered on and on about the movie stars who were her customers. "This is quite a coincidence," she added, after handing Wally back her credit card and copying down her name and address so Wally could be added to the mailing list, "because I was just about to call Ms. Jensen and tell her about the shipment of Egyptian scarabs that came in today. I know she'll love them." She indicated the showcase the new merchandise was in. "You know, I just realized you live in the town where her latest movie is being filmed. Have you met her?"

"Um, s-sort of," Wally sputtered. If the woman only knew. She cleared her throat. "Please excuse me, it's just that my throat is a little sore and I'm feeling chilled. I can't wait to get home to go to bed."

The saleswoman looked at her closely. "You're right, you do look a little funny. Maybe before you get on the highway for that long drive you should stop in the little tea shop down the street and have some tea with honey. It always helps my throat when I'm sick."

"I'll do exactly that," Wally said. "Thanks."

Wally hurried over to the tea shop all the while thinking about Jensen's lies. Whether it was enough to convince the authorities that Nancy was innocent was doubtful. She had to find a link between Jensen and the actual poison.

She was so lost in thought, the waitress had to ask for her order twice. "Have a seat anywhere," the teenaged girl said. "I'll bring it to you in a minute."

The shop was charming, with frilly curtains on the windows and starched white tablecloths, but quite cold. Other patrons, though, seemed warm enough in shirt sleeves. Wally was beginning to fear she was coming down with something and that made her all the more eager to figure out how she could back up her theories quickly.

From what Dominique had told her about the interview she and Elliot had conducted, she knew Jensen cooked simple, basic food. Her exact words, according to the detective, were, "nothing exotic." Something about that statement had been bothering Wally. Simple broiled fish and vegetables, she'd said, but her husband, Tim, had said something else at the party. Wally wished she could remember what it was.

She sipped her tea and tried to remember. Suddenly she had it. He'd said Beverly's California rolls were almost as good as Melanie's. So Jensen didn't just broil fish. Maybe she did even more than that. Maybe she not only made California rolls, but also made sushi. And maybe she knew a lot more about fish than she'd let on.

It wasn't much, but Wally thought her theories might at least help the police believe enough to search for the bracelet and maybe find traces of the poison in it. As soon as she got back to her car, she planned to call Elliot and Dominique with the information.

By the time she left the shop, after another pot of tea, the sky was completely overcast. A few fat snowflakes fell but melted on the sidewalks which had been warmed in the sun. Even so, the more Wally walked, the colder it got. Worse, once she got to her car she found she had left her cellphone home, charging on the kitchen counter.

The wind picked up, gusting a bit, and then blew steadily from the northwest. The clouds darkened. Wally made it back to the road leading to the highway before the blizzard hit, and was able to continue driving only by following the tail-lights of the car in front.

The wipers did little to keep the windows clear. Wally gritted her teeth as her little car slipped and skidded along the road. She thought she was almost at the highway, but it was so difficult to see she couldn't be sure until she saw the big green sign.

A large all-terrain vehicle loomed up beside her as she approached the entrance ramp. Since the road was so slippery, Wally pulled further right to make sure she didn't slide into the other car. It pulled right, too, making it hard for her to stay on the road. She slowed, letting it move ahead of her. It would be much easier to find her way, she knew, if she had the big car's headlights to lead her.

But the SUV slowed too. Wally strained to see inside but the driver's head was swaddled in scarves. Large sunglasses made eye contact impossible.

Shaking off the tension, Wally sped up, turning her wheel further right. With a sickening crunch, she felt the other car bang into her door. It bounced off but immediately hit her again. Then there was a clunk as her right front tire hit some hidden hazard, making her stamp on the brakes. That sent her into a skid, which ended with her barely avoiding some trees off the side of the road.

The other car, instead of slowing to see if she was okay, sped up. Snow churned from the tires, covering Wally's side window before she could see the license plate. She was left alone.

Her own tires spun. No amount of rocking could move the car. She needed help. Turning on her flashers, she turned off the car and got out, looking for a place to hang her red wool scarf to signal her trouble. But there was no antenna and there was no way to tie anything to her car door handles. The best thing she could do was hang her scarf out the window, which let the howling wind inside the car. Wally pulled her coat close around her in an attempt to keep warm. But the sight of all that snow made her shivers worse.

Her throat felt so scratchy. She closed her eyes for just a minute, hopeful that the pounding in her head would stop. But it continued, getting louder and louder.

Someone knocked on the window. "Hey, is anyone in there?" a voice asked, after clearing the snow from the driver's window.

Wally struggled to clear her head as she opened the door, sending a cascade of snow off it onto the white covered ground. "Here."

"Are you all right?" a uniformed police officer asked. "It looks like you had a collision."

"I did. Did you find the car that hit me?"

"There have been a lot of accidents today, ma'am."

Wally was sure it was no accident, but she didn't think the officer would believe her.

"Do you need a tow?"

"Maybe just a push. I think the car is still drivable."

Another officer joined him and helped get Wally's car off the side and back onto the road. They pronounced it safe to drive and gave her a number to call for the police report.

"How did you ever find me?" she asked, looking around and noticing that the entire landscape was white.

"The highway patrol finally got around to clearing this road. They saw your car and called it in. You had better get home. Do you have far to go?" he asked.

"Uhhh . . ." She wasn't able to come up with a reasonable response.

"Are you okay? You don't look well."

Wally felt awful, but she struggled to make sense of the situation. "Are you sure the road is clear?" she asked.

"It isn't snowing much now," the cop said. "You should be okay. Do you need to call anyone?"

Wally thought about it. Nate wouldn't be home yet. Her head had begun to throb again and this decision-making was almost more than she could handle. "Call Dominique Scott or Elliot Levine, Grosvenor, New Jersey police department," she said, as best as her throat could handle. "They'll take care of it. Just tell them Wally is on the way."

"Yes, ma'am."

The snow may have stopped but the roads were a mess. The right and middle lanes moved impossibly slowly and the left lane was a sheet of ice. Wally didn't dare go into it because there were cars stuck every quarter-mile or so that reminded her that she could easily skid off onto the median.

The roads in New York and New Jersey were somewhat better, though, and Wally was able to relax her stranglehold on the steering wheel. Yet it was after nine when she got home, dehydrated and feverish. Nate was standing at the

window and ran out as soon as she turned into the driveway.

"You look awful," he said, not even mentioning the car.
"Get into bed and I'll bring up some soup."

"Second shelf in the freezer," she said automatically.

"I'm opening a can. Do you want anything else?"

"Two hundred aspirin and a giant hot water bottle."

Nate felt her head and blew on his hand like he'd been
burned. "I'll see what I can find."

She was almost asleep when Nate brought her soup.

"I have to tell Dominique and Elliot," she said, when she
finished her soup.

"Tomorrow."

"No, now, it's important."

"Tomorrow," Nate said firmly. He pulled the covers up
on her side of the bed. "Go to sleep." He turned out the
light on his way out of the room. Wally was too sick and
too tired to try to make the call. Tomorrow would be fine.

Chapter Twenty-two

W ally's head felt so heavy when she awoke at eleven the next morning that she had to carefully roll out of bed and hope that gravity wouldn't slam it down to the floor as soon as it left the safety of the pillow. She practically crawled into the bathroom to wash her face, and felt little better on the way back to bed.

"You look terrible," Nate said.

Wally closed her eyes to keep out the glare of the sun reflecting off the new snow that was coming through her bedroom window. "I feel like something the dog spit out."

Nate tucked the comforter up near Wally's chin. "You poor thing. I'll stay with you if you want."

"What about your office?"

"It's closed. Cassie is still sick; I think you have what she has. And there is too much snow for anyone to come over. I can answer most of the calls from here and there will be several, based on what the radio says. There was a lot of damage during the storm."

Wally remembered skidding across the lanes on the highway and shuddered. She wasn't ready to tell Nate how the car got damaged, though. "The storm was bad."

"Yes. And dangerous. How could you go up there with a storm coming?"

"I didn't know it was really going to snow."

He shook his head, then fluffed her pillow. "Did you find out anything?"

Wally nodded, which was a huge mistake. She had to grab her head to keep it from splitting open. When the pain ebbed, she asked, "Did anyone call?"

"Dominique did. She wanted to see how you were feeling."

"How did she know I was sick?"

"Elliot called her last night when you got home." Nate felt her head. "Your fever is down. Can I bring you some tea and toast?"

"That sounds good." Wally snuggled down under the covers and wished she was wearing socks. Her feet were like ice. "Could you just hand me the phone before you go?"

Nate looked disapproving, but gave it to her.

"Take your time," Wally said, as she dialed the police station.

Dominique picked up on the first ring. Wally asked if Elliot was around too, but he was out, helping with some snow-related problems. "Did you get anything?" she asked.

"Well, yes and no." Wally filled her in on her sushi theory. Then she said, "I think I know how Melanie carried the poison into the party." She told her about the bracelet and the saleswoman's claim that she had sold Jensen one just like it. "You should see if you can find it on the videotape, or in one of the photos of Melanie at the party."

"Okay, we'll look. Anything else?"

Wally took a deep breath to try to steady her jumpy nerves. "When I left the town, a car tried to force me off the road. Correction, a car did force me off the road."

Dominique gasped. "That's it. You aren't doing anymore investigating."

"We still have no proof about the motive," Wally reminded her. "Or the source of the poison."

"Nevertheless, you have to stay out of it." Dominique sounded firm. "Promise me."

Wally agreed. She wasn't going anywhere now, anyway. A nap seemed to be in order.

When she woke up later, Debbie was sitting in the chair near the window. She pulled Wally's comforter up closer to her chin. "Get some rest, and I'll bring you soup."

"Not another canned soup, okay?"

Debbie shook her head and smiled. "I'll defrost some for you."

"I'm so glad you agreed to see me here," Wally said, after another bout of coughing. "I can't believe you make house calls in this day and age." She coughed again, weakly. "It's really too far to go all the way to Manhattan to see you."

Doug Cohen smiled as he folded up his stethoscope and handed her three prescriptions. "Most of my patients live or work in Manhattan. But you aren't one of my patients. Why didn't you call your own doctor?"

"I really wanted to see you," Wally admitted, "to see how you are doing."

"I'm all right. We're getting by."

Assessing the dark rings under his eyes, Wally wondered how true that was. She didn't question him, though, at least not about that. "I had hoped to hear from you about whose file Beverly might have seen."

Doug shifted his weight but stayed silent.

"It was Melanie Jensen's," Wally said softly, "wasn't it?"

Without acknowledging her statement, Doug closed his medical bag and shrugged on his cashmere topcoat. "I have to go."

Wally got up and went over to her bedroom door and closed it, standing steadfastly in front of it, trying like crazy to appear taller than she was, and more imposing. "It was, wasn't it?"

Doug turned tortured eyes toward her. "Yes."

"And her file showed that she was never pregnant," Wally pressed, "didn't it?"

"Why would you think that?"

Wally didn't answer directly. "It showed that she couldn't have children, and I'm guessing, based on the way she looked as an androgynous teenager before she retired, and the way she looked all rounded and filled out when she returned to acting, that she may have been a hermaphrodite."

The doctor looked at her in surprise, but kept his mouth shut.

"I thought so," Wally said, relaxing back down to her normal stature, and allowing another cough to escape her. "I've been doing a lot of research on the internet. It has happened to other people, but they don't kill over it."

Doug seemed to squirm. "I'm not confirming anything. But just consider this—not everyone has it handled at an appropriate time or sensitively. There are still some ignorant baby doctors in the backwaters of this country. It can be a traumatic thing to learn as a teenager."

Wally stared at him. "Do you know what you're saying? That it's okay that Melanie killed Beverly to keep her from confirming her problem to Tad Seymour? It's alright because the whole thing was upsetting for her?"

"Look, I'm not saying you are right or wrong, but it's no one's business but her family's."

Wally nodded. "I agree completely. But she killed your wife, probably so the family wouldn't find out."

"I don't believe that. How would she get her hands on that poison?"

"I think she makes her own sushi," Wally said, coughing into her fist. With difficulty, because of the choking congestion, she added, "Maybe she knows a lot about fish."

Finally Doug reacted the way Wally would have expected the widower of a murder victim to react. "You're right! She mentioned it once when I was warning her about mercury levels." His face got very red. "She killed her! How could she? I loved that woman."

"Beverly?"

"Yes, of course. Who else?"

"Well, I just, uh . . . ." Wally clamped her lips shut, wishing she had thought to do that before she opened her mouth.

The puzzled look faded from Doug's face. "Oh, you mean Janet. I love her too. But not the same way. Our marriage won't be the same."

"So you're getting married?" Wally realized she should have figured that would happen. Doug was so weak-willed. He'd have no chance up against Janet Finkelman. Those poor children.

"Yes, I guess so. I was waiting . . . for sufficient time to elapse."

A deeper truth struck Wally. "You were also waiting to make sure that Janet didn't kill Bev, weren't you?"

"Yes," Doug said quietly. "I feel so guilty about cheating on her, and for a while I really thought that Janet . . . ."

Wally put her hand on his arm. "I understand. We have to tell the police about Melanie."

Doug straightened up, but his face was grim. "I can't reveal anything about a patient."

"Then we'll have to get a confession, or somehow connect her to the poison."

"How?"

Wally gestured at the telephone, while coughing into her other hand. "I'm waiting for confirmation from the police about the fugu connection. Possibly they can get someone to admit selling it to her. If we get that, we should have a good chance. Let's keep our fingers crossed."

Doug reminded her about the prescription he'd written for cough medicine. "You're going to be just fine," he said as he picked up his doctor's bag and walked to the door. "Take lots of fluids."

"Take care of yourself," Wally said, hoping he would someday recover from his wife's murder.

The next time the phone rang Wally had her final confirmation. It was Dominique.

"Sorry I took so long to get back to you," she said. "I had to get assistance from the FDA. But we got lucky! We found a fish merchant in Boston and he gave us a statement."

Gripping the phone, Wally exclaimed, "That's it! I knew it."

"We also took a statement from the saleswoman at that store you went to, and she not only verified that Melanie bought a bracelet like the one you described, but she also said that she called Melanie just after you left to tell her about some jewelry and mentioned that you had been in the store."

"Did she tell Melanie she had sent me to the tea shop?"

"Yes."

"You think Melanie is the one who tried to run me off the road?"

"It's possible," Dominique said. "We're planning to try to find out. But we still don't have confirmation about that other thing."

"Yes, we do." Wally explained as quickly as she could about Doug's visit, punctuating it all with repeated coughs. She was exhausted by the coughing, and positively sore in her stomach muscles from the effort. But she continued. "Doug Cohen can't exactly confirm it and it wouldn't do any good anyway. Motive isn't enough. We need evidence. Do we have enough if she won't make a confession?"

The detective sounded confident. "We'll get it. I've put in a request for a search warrant, so we can look for the bracelet."

"Wouldn't she have thrown it out?"

"If she did, we'll get a warrant to search the garbage dump her town uses. We're also going to check her cars while we're searching her house. We want to see if there is any connection to the green paint Elliot found on your car. He's so angry, he has even volunteered to be the one who goes through the dump looking for the bracelet if it comes to that."

"He should make those county people do it with him. They were sure it was Nancy."

"Maybe he will."

Wally hung up and coughed for several minutes. The effort left her aching and exhausted, but satisfied. Now she could convalesce in peace.

Epilogue

"**D**id you get the book?" Wally asked as Louise came through her back door and sat down at the kitchen table. She placed a glass of iced tea and some cookies in front of her friend immediately, a mandatory drink on such a hot September day.

"I got the first copy they took out of the box," Louise said after taking a big sip of her tea. "They barely had time to ring it up before I got back to my car."

Wally looked at the book her friend had pulled out of the bag. There it was, in black and white—the book by H. Seltzer that was the tell-all about Melanie Jensen.

"Look," Louise said, flipping to the back cover. "It's him, your stalker."

A picture of the man Wally knew as Tad Seymour stared back at her. He didn't look nearly as down on his luck anymore. It still amazed her that Melanie Jensen had given his alter ego—Hyman Seltzer—the exclusive story, about her teenage anguish and her lapse of sanity, as she called it, regarding Beverly Cohen. Seymour's attempts to get the story published were directly responsible for Jensen murdering his source, and therefore somewhat responsible for the predicament she was in, yet she spilled her innermost secrets to him. It was amazing.

"It's going to bring it all up again," Wally said.

Louise smiled. "Especially when he goes on Oprah. I wonder if they'll have Melanie on satellite from prison. It's the only way she'll ever be on television again."

That was probably true, Wally thought. Melanie Jensen had been sentenced to twenty-five-years-to-life. "That whole family has been devastated," she said. "Those poor children." She stood up and got Louise a refill.

Louise shook her head and helped herself to another cookie. "Not so poor. I read an article last week about them and their father, and how they're dealing with all of it. Tim is a wonderful father, and he is standing behind Melanie, even though he knew nothing about her medical problems, the artificial insemination of the surrogate, or the murder. If only she had been honest from the beginning, none of it would have happened."

Wally was surprised that Louise knew so much about it. She had heard something similar, about Tim saying that although he abhorred what Melanie did, he still loved his wife. Maybe if Melanie had known how he truly felt, she would have opened up to him.

"I just hope we don't have newspeople swarming all over the place again," Wally said.

Louise nodded. "You're not the only one, but I guess it's been the worst for you."

Wally rolled her eyes. It had been awful. The media stopped paying attention to Nancy Goldstein after she was cleared and her family life went back to normal. They wouldn't be affected by another wave of publicity, since they had already moved to Texas, where Nancy's husband's new job was located. But Wally, who had been hounded by reporters for days after Jensen's arrest, and again during the trial when she appeared as a witness, did not look forward to seeing her face plastered on the news again.

"The book has a good cover," Louise said. "And there are lots of pictures inside. I peeked when I was at a traffic light." She opened to a picture of the cast of the cancelled movie, *Stalking Sunrise*. "It's too bad they didn't finish the movie. The people in town who were supposed to be paid for the use of their property are out a lot of money."

It was a mess, Wally agreed. "But Shariah Jones and Kevin Cole both landed new movies right away, I heard."

Louise stared at her, then narrowed her eyes. "Oh, sorry, I didn't notice your new haircut."

Wally laughed. Her friend knew her well—she only heard about that kind of stuff in the hair salon. "And there is a new campaign for Viceroy cologne," she added knowledgeably. "So Heath Maxwell's doing okay."

"You still like things tied up neatly, don't you?" Louise asked. "No loose ends?"

Wally nodded. "It's the only way."